"I'm trying to prove I found the right answer to the puzzle."

Joe nodded, frowning thoughtfully at the same time. "So tell me, am I the answer or the puzzle?"

Kelly grinned at him. "Both right now."

He looked down at her eyes, and he was suddenly overwhelmed with the urge to kiss her. Would she stop him?

What if he took her in his arms and held her close and let his male instincts come back to life…?

Reaching out, he slipped his hand behind her head, his fingers in her hair, and began to pull her toward him.

For the moment she was his for the asking. But what gave him the right to be asking? This wasn't the way it should be. She deserved better. She deserved real love, and that was something he couldn't give her…

Dear Reader

When I think of San Diego, I think of rainbows and pastel colours, contrasted with the deep blue of the sea and the bright gold of the sun. Boats and beaches and suntanned bodies. It's a city of dreams and transitions. Cultures don't clash here—they meet and blend together in a magic way. For some, dreams do come true.

Kelly Vrosis comes to San Diego aching for validation. She not only earns that, but ends up finding an honest-to-goodness Prince Charming and losing her heart. But what good does it do a normal, ordinary girl from the Heartland to fall in love with a prince—especially one who is just beginning to test his royal prerogatives? Sounds like a blueprint for heartbreak, doesn't it?

Ah, but there is another factor involved—a tiny little girl with huge dark eyes, a big gaping need for a mommy and a daddy, and a heart damaged by the past. Will she accept Kelly and learn to trust her daddy, the Prince? If only she can, all their dreams might come true.

I have faith! How about you?

Raye Morgan

SINGLE FATHER, SURPRISE PRINCE!

BY
RAYE MORGAN

First published in Great Britain 2010
Harlequin Mills & Boon Limited,
Eton House, 18-24 Paradise Road, Richmond, Surrey TW9 1SR

ISBN: 978 0 263 21560 1

Harlequin Mills & Boon policy is to use papers that are natural,
renewable and recyclable products and made from wood grown in
sustainable forests. The logging and manufacturing process conform
to the legal environmental regulations of the country of origin.

Printed and bound in Great Britain
by CPI Antony Rowe, Chippenham, Wiltshire

Raye Morgan has been a nursery school teacher, a travel agent, a clerk and a business editor, but her best job ever has been writing romances—and fostering romance in her own family at the same time. Current score: two boys married, two more to go. Raye has published over seventy romances, and claims to have many more waiting in the wings. She lives in Southern California, with her husband and whichever son happens to be staying at home at the moment.

This book is dedicated to Julie in San Diego

CHAPTER ONE

SOMEONE WAS WATCHING him. Joe Tanner swore softly, tilted his face into the California sun and closed his eyes. A stalker. He could feel the eyes focused on the sun-baked skin right between his bare shoulder blades.

He'd spent enough time as an Army Ranger in the jungles of Southeast Asia avoiding contact with snipers to know when someone had him in his sites. When you'd developed a sixth sense like that just to keep yourself alive, you didn't forget how to use it.

"Just like riding a bicycle," he muttered to himself, opening his eyes and turning to see if he could filter out where the person was watching from.

He'd first noticed the interest he was getting from someone—someone possibly hostile—the day before, but he hadn't paid a lot of attention. Joe knew he was tall and tanned and reasonably good-looking, with thick brown hair tipped blond by the sun, and he seldom passed unnoticed by onlookers wherever he went. He'd assumed it was basically a casual surveillance. Living half his day wearing nothing but board shorts, he was used to having his half-naked body studied by strangers. He knew he had interesting scars.

Besides, he had other things on his mind. Someone was arriving tonight—someone from his old life, although he'd never met her. He was nervous. So he'd been thinking about important changes that were coming, and he'd ignored the lurker.

It wasn't until today that he began to get that creepy shiver of caution down his spine. When the hair on the back of his neck started to rise, he knew it was time to give this situation due diligence. Better safe than sorry, after all.

His gaze swept the San Diego beach. Though there was a fog bank threatening to come ashore, it was a fairly warm day and the usual suspects were flocking in for the waves and the atmosphere—the surfers, the moms chasing little children across the sand, the hobos hoping for a handout. The flirty beach girls were also out in full force—a curvaceous threesome of that variety were lingering close right now, giggling and smiling at him hopefully. There'd been a time when he would have smiled right back, but those days were long gone.

You could at least be friendly, a little voice inside his head complained. He ignored it. What was the point? It only encouraged them. And he had nothing for them, nothing at all.

He gave them a curt nod, but moved his attention on, searching the storefronts, the frozen-banana stand, the tourist shop with the slightly risqué T-shirts, the parking lot where a young, swimsuit-clad couple stood leaning against a sports car, wrapped in each other's fervent embrace, looking as though the world were about to end and they had to get a lifetime's worth of kissing in before it did.

Young love. He had a sudden urge to warn them, to tell them not to count on each other or anything else in this life. Everyone had to make it on his own. There were no promises, no guidelines to depend on. There was only Murphy's Law—anything that can go wrong will go wrong. You could count on that, at least. Be prepared.

But he wisely passed up the chance to give them the advantage of his unhappy experiences. Nobody ever listened, anyway. Everybody seemed to have to learn the hard way.

So who was it that was causing the hair on the back of his neck to bristle? The blind beggar in the faded Hawaiian shirt, sitting out in the sun on a little wooden stool next to his wise old collie? That hardly seemed likely. The cop making lazy passes down the meandering concrete walkway on his bicycle? No, he was watching everyone in a thoroughly professional manner, as he always did. The bag lady throwing out bread crusts to the raucous and ravenous sea gulls? The teenager practicing acrobatic tricks on his skateboard?

No. None of these.

As time ticked by, he began to settle on one lonely figure, and as he zeroed in, the way his pulse quickened told him he was right.

The person was lurking alongside the wall that separated the walkway from the sand. Joe pulled his sunglasses off the belt of his swim shorts and jammed them in front of his eyes so that he could watch the watcher without seeming to be looking in that direction. The culprit was wearing a thick sweatshirt with the hood pulled low, baggy jeans caked with wet sand around the feet, so it was difficult at first glance to see the gender he was dealing with. But it took only seconds of focused attention to realize the truth—this was a woman pretending to be a boy.

That only sharpened his sense of danger. His military experience had taught him that the most lethal threats often came wrapped in the most benign-looking packages. Never trust pretty women or adorable kids.

Turning as though scoping out the activity at the nearby marina, he watched from the corner of his eye as the woman slipped down to sit on the low wall, pulling a small notebook out of the front pocket of the sweatshirt and jotting something in it before stowing it away again.

Yup. It was her all right. And she was keeping notes. So what now?

He considered his alternatives. Direct confrontation was usually counterproductive. She would just deny that she had any interest in him at all, and slink away.

And then what? Very likely, whoever had sent her would just send someone else. Another case of treating the symptom instead of the cause. His curiosity had been aroused now. He wanted to know who was behind this and why.

The only way to make a real attempt at getting to the bottom of the situation would be to get to her some-how—earn her trust, maybe. Get her to talk. But first he would have to draw her out, force her into making a move that would prove her intent.

And why not? He had nothing better to do for the next hour or so of his life.

With a shrug, Joe leaned down to pick up his surf-board, and started toward the next pier. It was under-going renovation and there were signs posted warning people to stay away. Nice and out of the way, with most of the beach crowd focused in another direction, it would be perfect.

He trudged through the sand, letting his natural in-clination exaggerate the slight limp he still had from the leg that was only beginning to fully heal after almost a year of recuperation.

He didn't even turn to see if she was following. He just assumed she would be. The type who tried to mess with his life always followed the script to the letter, and he had no doubt she would do the same.

Kelly Vrosis bit her lip as she watched the man who called himself Joe Tanner start walking. She saw where he was headed—way off the beaten path. Her heart began to thump in her chest. Should she follow him? She was going to have to if she was going to do this thing right, wasn't she?

She only had one week, and she'd already wasted a day and a half not daring to get close enough to really do anything observant. Either she was going to document all Joe Tanner's activities and figure out if he was who she thought he was, or she wasn't, and she'd wasted a lot of time and credibility on a wild-goose chase. Taking a deep breath, she fingered the little digital camera hidden in her pocket, and rose slowly to her feet, ready to do what had to be done.

"Here goes," she muttered to herself, and then started off down the beach, staying higher, closer to the storefronts, trying to be as invisible as possible, but still keep the tall, muscular figure of the man she was following in sight.

She was pretty sure he hadn't noticed her. She wasn't the sort who usually got noticed in crowds, and she'd worked hard on an outfit that would keep her anonymous.

Yesterday, after she'd driven out from the airport and checked into a motel room close to the address she'd found for Joe, she'd walked by his little beach house twice, so nervous she'd thought she couldn't breathe as she went quickly past his gate. She had no idea what she would do when she finally came face-to-face with the man she'd been researching for months now. The whole thing had become ridiculously emotional for her. Oh Lord, what if she passed out?

She didn't really expect that to happen, but it was true that there was something about him that sent her pulse racing—though she would never have admitted it to her coworkers, who had tried to talk her out of coming.

She worked as an analyst at a bureau in Cleveland, Ohio, the Ambrian News Agency. A child of Ambrian parents herself, she was fast becoming an expert in all things Ambrian. The little island nation of her ancestry wasn't well-known, especially under the current xenophobic regime. She'd taken as her special area of expertise the children of the monarchy that had been overthrown twenty-five years before.

It was recorded that they all had been killed that night of the coup, along with their parents, the king and queen. But now there was some question as to whether a few may have survived. And when she'd opened the national newsmagazine almost a year ago now and caught sight of a picture of Joe Tanner, returning war hero, she'd gasped in immediate recognition.

"Ohmigosh! He looks just like… Oh, it can't be! But he sure does look like…"

She knew it was nuts right from the beginning, and everyone she worked with agreed.

So she'd dug into the life of Joe Tanner and used all the resources available to her at the agency to find out all she could. Meanwhile, she became one of the top experts on the royal children. She knew everything about them that was to be known. And a few things that weren't. And she became more and more obsessed.

Now here she was, testing out her theory in real time. And scared to death to actually talk to the man.

It wasn't like her to be such a ninny. She'd grown up with two brothers and usually had an easy time dealing with men on the whole, but ever since she'd caught sight of Joe's face in that magazine article, she'd put him in a special category. She knew he was an extraordinary man, from what she'd read about him. He'd done things—and survived things—that no one she knew had ever done. What was he going to do when he realized that she was prying into his life?

"Kelly, you can't do this," Jim Hawker, the older man

who was her boss and office mate, had warned when she confided her plan to him. "You're letting a wacky obsession take over your common sense. You took one look at that picture and your overactive imagination created a huge conspiracy around it."

"But what if I'm right?" she'd insisted passionately. "I have to go to California and see what I can find out. I've got two weeks of vacation. I've got to see for myself."

Jim had grimaced. "Kelly, you're going to be annoying a man who has done things to people with his bare hands that you couldn't imagine in your worst nightmares. If he really is who you think he is, what makes you think he's going to be happy that you figured it out? Let it go. It's a crazy theory anyway."

"It's not crazy. It's way out, I'll admit. But it's not crazy. Just think how important it could be to the Ambrian community if I'm right."

"Even if you're right, you'll be poking a tiger with a stick. Without the blessings of the agency, you'll be all alone. No backup." He shook his head firmly. "No, Kelly. Don't do it. Go to Bermuda. Take a cruise. Just stay away from California."

But she couldn't stay away from California. She had to find out if she was right. She'd promised Jim she would be very careful. And she wouldn't approach the man himself until she was sure of how she would be received.

Of course, once she'd arrived it had all turned out to be a lot harder than she'd bargained for. She'd picked him out of a crowd right away, but she'd begun to realize she wasn't going to find out much just by observing him.

She needed more—and time was short. That morning she'd spent an hour watching him surf, all the while trying to map out a plan. She was going to have to interrogate people who knew him.

Well, maybe not "interrogate." More like "chat with." She'd already begun to make a list of likely contacts, including the man who ran the little produce store on the corner of his block. The two had seemed quite friendly as she'd caught sight of Joe buying a bag of fruit there on his way home the night before. Then there was the model-pretty girl who lived in the tiny beach cottage next door to his. She'd positioned herself to say hello to him twice already, and though he didn't seem to respond with a lot of enthusiasm, he did smile. She might know something. He didn't seem to throw those smiles around too freely.

And what a smile he had. It made Kelly shiver a little just to remember it, and it hadn't even been aimed at her.

There were also the neighbors on the other side of his house—two college students who shared an apartment in the two-story building. She'd seen him talking to them as they got their racing bikes out that morning, so they might know something. She'd worn shorts and a T-shirt and jogged slowly up and down his street early enough to be rewarded with that glimpse of his day. Then she'd watched as he walked off toward the beach, surfboard tucked under his arm, and she'd quickly donned her current baggy outfit to keep him from noticing that he might have seen her before.

This had been a lot of work, and so far, she'd reaped

very little in the way of rewards. Despite her trepidation, she was feeling a little grumpy. She'd hoped for more.

Kelly kept her distance, continuing to skirt the beach by staying up near the buildings. But she noticed they were mostly boarded up now. The stores had petered out into a semi-industrial area, and it looked as though this whole section of shore had been condemned for demolition and renovation. She glanced around, noting that no one seemed to be about.

And then she looked back at where Joe had been walking.

Wait a minute. She froze. She'd lost him.

She hesitated, realizing she'd last sighted him just before he'd gone behind an old fishing boat someone had hauled up onto the sand. She'd spent a moment of inattention gazing out at the ocean, then at the old buildings.

So where was he? He couldn't have stopped there.

Had he gone under the closed pier? There was more beach on the other side and she waited a moment, searching for him, expecting him to pop out and continue walking on across the empty sand, but he didn't.

There was no one on that side of the pier. The shore turned rocky there, and a fog was rolling in—a bad combination for surfers. Why was he carrying his board if he didn't plan to surf? To keep it safe, she supposed, but it seemed a long way around. Where was he going, anyway?

Glancing back at where she'd begun, she frowned. The sun still shone and people still swarmed the sidewalks, but they looked faraway now. The scene ahead seemed still and eerie.

What should she do now?

Kelly pressed her lips together. She had to keep going. She didn't want to have to waste a lot of time staking out his house again and hoping he'd appear, as she had the day before. Too boring and very little payoff. Now that she had a fix on him, it would be better to keep on the trail right here and now.

Except he'd disappeared behind a boat or under a pier.

With a sigh, she started off. She was going to have to find out which.

The wet sand felt cold against her bare feet. The fog was rolling in fast, and there was no longer any evidence that a sun existed at all. She walked quickly around the old boat, eyeing the peeling paint and barnacles. No sign of Joe. She was going to have to walk under the pier.

She wrinkled her nose. The place was hardly inviting. Dark and dank and creaking, it smelled bad and looked worse. Shadows hid too many angles from view. Crabs scurried from one piling to another. Even the water had a scummy look.

Kelly paused, peering toward the beach, wondering where he could have gone. The fog was too thick to see far. She was going to have to walk through to the other side to really see anything. An eerie foghorn sounded off the shore, completing the strange ocean feel.

Wasn't this the way most murder mysteries began?

She hesitated a moment longer. Did she really have to do this? Couldn't she just go back the way she'd come?

Anyone with any sense would be on her way already. But Kelly was still going. This was what she'd come for....

With another sigh, she stepped under the crumbling supports of the pier, walking quickly to get it over with. Each step took her farther from the light and sank her more deeply into the cold and clammy gloom. She tried to keep her attention on the hints of daylight ahead. Just a few more steps and she would be out....

When the hand came shooting out of nowhere and yanked her hood off her head, she gasped and stumbled in surprise.

"So you *are* a girl," a rough voice said. "What the hell do you want?"

The shock sent her reeling. She couldn't scream, and her legs weren't working right. She looked up frantically, her heart in her throat, trying to see who this was.

Joe Tanner, the man she'd been following? Or someone else, someone more sinister?

This wasn't how she'd planned it. She wasn't ready. She could hardly make him out in the gloom, and wasn't sure if this was the man she had spun her theories about or not. Whoever he was, he was just too big and too overwhelming. Everything in her rebelled, and mindlessly, Kelly turned and ran toward daylight.

Although she felt as if she was screaming, she didn't hear a sound. Only the crunch of sand under her feet, her breath coming fast, and finally, the grunt as he tackled her and threw her to the beach, his hard body coming down on top of hers.

A part of her felt complete outrage. How dare he do this to her?

Yet another part felt nothing but fear. The way the fog had closed in around them, she knew no one had seen what he'd done. She couldn't hope for help from a passerby—not even a cell phone call to the police. It was as though they were in their own world. Jim's warning flashed in her head: *You don't want to be alone with this guy when he realizes you're studying him.*

Her mind frantically searched for all the lost details of that women's survival course she'd taken three years ago. Where were those pressure points again?

"Who are you?" His hand was bunched in the fabric of her sweatshirt. "Why are you tailing me?"

She sighed and closed her eyes for a few seconds, catching her breath. At least he hadn't hurt her. For now, he wanted to talk, not wrestle. Straining to turn her head so that she could see around the edge of her hood, she looked at the man who had her pinned to the ground with the weight of his body, and she saw what she'd been hoping to see.

Yes, this was Joe Tanner. Relief flooded her and she began to relax, but then she remembered Jim's warning again. Kelly was in an odd situation. She knew Joe had no right to treat her like this—but what was she going to do about it?

"Could you let me up?" she asked hopefully.

"Not until I know why you've got me staked out."

"I don't," she protested, but her cheeks were flaming.

"Liar."

He hadn't hurt her and something told her he wasn't going to. She began to calm down. Now the major emotion she was feeling was embarrassment. She should have handled this in a more professional manner. Here she was, lying on the beach with the subject of her investigation. Not cool. She hoped Jim and the others at the office never found out about it.

"You see, Kelly," she could almost hear Jim saying, *"I told you to leave these things to people who know what they're doing."*

Of course, she always made the obvious argument. "How am I ever going to learn how to do this right if you never let me try?" But no one took her seriously.

So here she was, trying, and learning—and messing up a little bit. But she would get better. She gritted her teeth and promised herself that was what was happening here. She was getting better at this.

But she had to admit it wasn't easy to keep her mind on business with this man's incredible body pressed against hers, sending her pulse on a race. He was hard and smooth and golden—all things the perfect prince should be. Good thing she was covered from head to foot in sweatshirt material and denim, because he wasn't covered with much at all.

"Come on," he was saying now. "I want to know who put you up to this." He sounded cold and angry and forceful enough to wipe out any thoughts of sensuality she might be dreaming up. "Who are you working for?"

"N-nobody."

Which was technically true. Her office hadn't author-ized this investigation. She was strictly on her own.

"Liar," he said again.

Reaching out, he pulled the hood all the way off her head, exposing her matted blonde curls. She turned her pretty face and large dark eyes his way and he frowned.

"What the hell?"

This young woman was hardly the battle-hardened little tough he'd expected. She was a greenhorn, no doubt about it. No one in his right mind would have sent her up against him.

A little alarm bell went off in the back of Joe's mind, reminding him about lowering guards and being lulled into complacency. But even that seemed ridiculous in this case. She was too soft, too cute, too…amateur. His quick survey of her nicely rounded body as he'd brought her down had told him she wasn't carrying a weapon, though she did have a couple of small, light objects in the front pockets of her sweatshirt.

He'd had plenty of experience in fighting off threats. He'd fought off hired guns, martial arts experts, Mata Hari types with vials of poison hidden in their bras. This little cutie didn't fit into any of those categories. He would have staked his life on her being from outside that world of intrigue he'd swum in for years. So what the hell was she doing here?

"I'm not 'tailing' you and I don't have you 'staked out,'" she insisted breathlessly.

He raised one sleek eyebrow, looking her over.

"Then it must be love," he said sarcastically. "Why

else would you be mooning around after me for days at a time?"

Shocked at the very suggestion, even though she knew he was just making fun of her, she opened her mouth to respond, but all that came out was a strangled sound.

"Never mind," he said in a kindly manner, though he was obviously still mocking her, and his mockery stung. "We'll just stay here this way until you remember what the answer is."

"To what?" she managed to choke out.

She tried to wriggle out from under him, but soon realized it was probably a mistake. She could see him better, but that only sent her nerves skittering like jumping beans on a hot plate.

He had hold of her sweatshirt and one strong leg was still thrown over hers. It was pretty clear he didn't like being followed. He was angry and he wanted the truth. Nothing amorous about it.

Still, he was just a little too gorgeous for comfort. She wasn't usually one to be tongue-tied, but being this close to him sent every sensible thought flying right out of her head. His huge blue eyes were gazing at her as though her skin were transparent and he could see everything—every thought, every feeling. She stared at him, spellbound, unable to move.

He began to look impatient.

"Let's cut to the chase," he said shortly. "I gave you your options. Pick one."

She licked her dry lips and had to try twice before she got out an actual word or two. "I…I can't."

"Why not?" he demanded. "I want the truth."

She shook her head, trying to clear it. What could she possibly say that he would understand at this point? All her explanations needed too much background. Despair began to creep into her thought processes.

"I have to get up," she told him. "If you don't release me, I'm going to get hysterical."

"Be serious," he scoffed. But then he looked at her a bit closer and what he saw seemed to convince him. Reluctantly, he rolled away.

"Women," he muttered darkly, but he let her get up, and he rose as well.

She took a deep breath and steadied herself. At least they were out from under that awful pier. The fog hid the sun, but the sand was still warm here and that was a bit comforting.

She looked up at him. He was all tanned skin and muscles, with sand sprinkled everywhere, even on his golden eyelashes. For a moment she was dazzled, but she quickly frowned and brought herself back down to earth. This was no time to let attraction take over. She had work to do.

"What's your name?" he demanded.

"Kelly Vrosis," she responded.

He almost smiled. That answer had been so quick, so automatic, he had no doubt it really was her name. What was going on here? Didn't she know she was supposed to lie about these things?

"Okay," he said. "I was nice to you. Your turn."

She opened her eyes wide, playing dumb. "What?"

she asked, shaking her head as though she didn't have a clue what he wanted from her.

He gave her a long-suffering look. "Okay, Kelly Vrosis. No more messing around. There are only three reasons people follow me. Some want information. Some want to stop me from doing something. But most want me dead." He pinned her with a direct stare. "So which is it?"

CHAPTER TWO

KELLY SHOOK HER HEAD, feeling a touch of panic. "None of those. Honest."

Joe's hard face looked almost contemptuous. "Then what?"

She glanced up at him and swallowed hard. She'd had a cover story ready when she'd started this. It had seemed a good one at the time—something about thinking he was her college roommate's brother—but now it just seemed lame. She had to admit this had turned out to be very different from what she'd expected or planned. Serious consequences loomed. This was scary.

"Uh, well…" she said, trying to buy time while she thought up something better. But then she stopped herself. There was no point in filling the air with nonsense just to give the impression she had something to say. He wasn't going to buy it, anyway.

Things were happening too quickly. She needed a moment to reflect, to stand back and look at this man and make a judgment call. Was he or was he not the man she theorized he had to be?

She'd put all of her credibility on the line, coming to

California and looking him up. Had she done something stupid? Or was she a genius?

Of course, she'd been crazy to get this close to him this early. She was on her own. If she got into trouble there would be no one to call.

Was she in trouble right now? Hard to tell. But it sure felt like it.

She looked him over. His blond-tipped hair was too long and sticking out at all angles. His skin was too tan. His body was too beautiful—and also too scarred to look at without wincing. He was barefoot and covered with sand. He didn't look like any prince she'd ever seen before.

Was she crazy? What if she was completely wrong? How could she have put herself and her career out on a limb like this? Maybe she should just pull back and rethink this whole thing.

"I saw you writing in a notebook," he said, moving toward her in a deliberate way that made her take a step backward. "It was about me, wasn't it?"

"What? No…" But she knew her face revealed the truth.

His clear blue eyes challenged her. "I want to see it."

Taking a deep breath, she tried for a bit of professionalism. She couldn't just roll over for this man.

"You have no right to see it. It's private property. My property."

"If it's about me, I think I have every right."

"No, you don't!"

"Hand it over."

"No."

"Never mind," he said impatiently, reaching for her. "We'll do it this way."

She wasn't certain what he had in mind, but was pretty sure she wasn't going to like it. She took another quick step backward.

"Wait." She put her hand to her mouth. "I think you chipped my tooth."

His first reaction was skepticism and she didn't blame him. It was a ploy, but she was desperate at this point.

"When?"

"When you tackled me."

To her surprise, he actually began to look concerned. "Here, let me see."

Moving forward and not giving her any room to maneuver, he took her face in his hands and looked down. This was a bit more than she'd bargained for. She wanted to protest, but after all, she'd set this up herself, hadn't she? And she really did feel a sharp edge on one of her upper fronts. Now she had to go through with it to prove her point. Tentatively, she opened her mouth.

"Here." She pointed at the place that felt sharp.

He leaned close, staring down. His hands were warm on her cheeks. His maleness overwhelmed her for a moment and she felt a bit light-headed. But his inspection didn't last long. He touched the tooth, then pulled back.

"As far as I can see, no tooth was injured during my expertly executed preemptive strike."

She gave him a look. "Cute," she said, exploring again with her tongue. "It feels chipped to me."

But while she was distracted, he was reaching to pull down the zipper of her sweatshirt, and that was another matter altogether.

"Hey," she cried, trying to jump away from his reach. "What do you think you're doing?"

"Checking," he said with calm confidence.

"Checking what?" She bristled with outrage.

"Don't worry. I've seen it all before." He gave her a sudden grin that just about knocked her backward on its own. "Just checking to see if you have a recorder on you. A bug. A mic."

She moved quickly to protect the little microcassette recorder tucked in the front pocket of her sweatshirt, but his hand was already sliding in there.

"Ah-hah." He pulled it out and waved it at her. "Just as I thought."

"Hey," she cried, truly indignant now, trying without success to snatch it back. "You can't do this."

He grinned again, eyes mocking as he dangled it just out of her reach. "Sue me."

And while she stretched to try to claim it, his other hand shot forward into her other pocket and snagged her notebook and her tiny digital camera.

"Give me back my things," she said, glaring at him, hands on her hips. A part of her was wincing, reminding her that she was reacting like any woman might, instead of like the intelligence agent she wanted to be. But she didn't have time to consider that. She couldn't let him do this!

"Okay now, this is just not fair."

"Not fair?" He set her items on a rock and stood in

front of them, so she knew she didn't have a chance to grab them unless he let her. "Life ain't fair, baby. Ya gotta learn to turn your lemons into lemonade."

Despite his obviously experience based advice, she wasn't ready to sign on to that attitude. She stuck her chin out and shot daggers at him with her eyes.

"You're bigger than I am. You're stronger than I am. You've got an unfair advantage. This isn't a fair fight."

He shrugged and took hold of the hood of her sweat-shirt on either side of her face so she couldn't escape, pulling her closer and gazing down into her eyes. Strangely, his look went from mocking to dreamy in less time than it took to think it. As she gazed into his blue eyes, he grazed her cheek with one palm, touching her as though he liked the feel of her skin.

"Who says we're fighting?" he said, his voice suddenly low and sensual.

As humiliating as it was to know that he could turn her reactions on and off like a switch, she couldn't seem to stop them. The seduction in his voice washed over her like a wave, turning her outrage into a sense of longing she'd never known before. All the blood seemed to drain from her head, and for a moment, she actually thought she was going to faint.

Kelly closed her eyes and summoned all her strength. Whatever was going on, she wouldn't let it happen.

"Oh, no, you don't," she said, trying to make her shaky voice firm as she looked at Joe again. "You think you can manipulate me like a puppy dog, don't you?"

He dropped his hand from her face and gave her a

pained look. "I see," he said, turning from her. "What we've got here is a drama queen."

She took a step after him. "Look, you've taken everything I brought with me. You proved you could do it." She put out her hand. "So can I have them back now?"

He shook his head. "Not yet." He hesitated, gazing at her speculatively. He'd already been through her sweatshirt pockets. All that was left were the pockets in her jeans. "What I'd like to see is some ID. Where's your wallet?"

"Oh, no, you don't," she repeated, backing away again. "You're not coming anywhere near these pockets."

His mouth twisted. "I suppose that would be going a step too far," he said with obvious regret.

"Even for you," she added. "Besides, you have no right to do any of this."

He shrugged. "Okay. Come on back here and sit down." He gestured toward the rock. "Let's take a look at what you've found out about me."

He was going to look through her research notes. She frowned, not sure what to do. If she didn't have a real need to get along with him, she would certainly be treating this invasion of her space quite differently. In fact, she might be willing to swear out a warrant right now.

"Sit down," he said again.

"Sorry," she said crisply. "I don't have time. I have to go find a policeman to have you arrested."

He looked at her for a moment, then rubbed his eyes tiredly. "Kelly, sit down."

She gazed at him defiantly. "No."

He gave her a world-weary, heavy-lidded look. "Do I have to tackle you again?"

She hesitated, watching as he sat on the long black rock and began to go through her things.

"Hey, you can't look at that," she said, stepping closer.

"I thought you were going to see if you could find a cop to stop me," he noted casually as he flipped through the pages of her notebook. "This is quite a little document of my life for the last two days," he noted. "But pretty boring."

"The truth hurts," she quipped.

His mouth twisted. That wasn't the only thing that hurt. The leg that had taken a bullet almost a year ago still wasn't totally healed. It ached right now. He'd been standing on it for too long.

And yet he was probably better off than he'd had any reason to hope he would be when he'd returned from overseas. He'd been torn and wounded, in soul as well as in body, and the bitterness over what had happened that last day in the Philippines still consumed him. That had always been worse than the physical pain. The bullets that had torn through the jungle that day had shattered his life, but the woman he loved had died in his arms.

Was that it? Was that what Kelly was after? Was she just another writer looking for a story? He eyed her speculatively.

At first he'd thought she must have worse things in mind. There were plenty of people from his past who might want to take him out. But he was pretty sure that wasn't what she'd come for. She wasn't the right type. And all this note taking suggested she was looking for information, not trying to do him actual harm. At least not at the moment.

In the VA hospital, there'd been a reporter who had hung around, wanting to know details, fishing for angles. He'd seen the article about the "returning heroes" that had featured Joe as well as a group of other men, and he'd sensed there was something more there. He'd wanted to write up Joe's story, wanted to use his life as fodder for a piece of sensational journalism. He hadn't actually known about Angie, but he'd known there had to be something.

Joe hadn't cooperated. In fact, things had gotten downright nasty there for awhile. There was no way he would allow Angie to be grist for anyone's mill. And anyway, the last thing guys like him needed was publicity. Something like that could destroy your usefulness, wipe out your career. If people knew who you were and what your game was, you were dead. Incognito was the way to go.

He was confronting this issue right now. His body was pretty much healed, but his mind? Not hardly. Was he going to be able to go back to work?

That was the question haunting him. He wasn't in the military any longer, but there were plenty of contractors who were ready to pay him a lot of money to do what he was doing before, only privately. And—let's face it—he didn't know much of anything else. But did he still have the heart for it? Had losing the woman he loved destroyed all that?

It hardly mattered. In just a few hours, his little girl—a little girl he'd never met—was arriving on a flight from the Philippines. He should be preparing for that. Once Mei was here, Joe had no idea what his life was going to be like. Everything had been on hold for months. Now he was about to see the future.

He still had no answers. But he knew one thing: he wasn't going to let anyone write about him. No way.

"So it *was* information you were aiming for after all," he said, paging through the notebook and feeling his annoyance begin to simmer into something else.

"Well, not really," she began, but he went on as though she hadn't spoken.

"Too bad you weren't around when I was smuggling contraband across the border," he said sardonically, looking up to where she was standing. "Or when I was inviting underaged girls over to my place for an orgy. Or hiding deserters in my rec room."

She finally slipped down to sit beside him in the rock. "I don't believe you ever did any of those things."

He winced. "Damn. I just can't get any respect anymore, can I?"

She gave him a baleful look. "You're wrong about me," she said calmly. "I'm not trying to dig up dirt on you."

His eyes were hooded and there was a hard line around his mouth. "No? Then what *are* you trying to do?"

She hesitated. What should she tell him? How much could she get away with and not let him know the truth? It was too soon to tell him everything. Much too soon.

And once he knew what she was here for, she had every reason to think that he would like her even less than he did now.

He was waving her notebook at her, his knuckles white. "This is me," he said, and to her surprise, his voice was throbbing with real anger. "You've taken a piece of me and you have no right to it."

She blinked, disconcerted that he was taking this so seriously. "But it's me, too. My writing."

"I don't care." He flipped the notebook open again and ripped the relevant pages out. Looking at her defiantly, he tore them into tiny pieces.

Her heart jumped but she held back her natural reaction. Something in the strength of his backlash warned her to let it be for now. Besides, she knew she hadn't written down anything very interesting as yet. It didn't really matter.

He dropped the scraps into her hand. "Let's see you try to put that back together again."

"Don't worry," she said brightly. "I don't need it. I can remember what I wrote."

"Really. Without this?" He held up her microcassette recorder. "And without this?" He added her tiny digital camera to the collection.

She bit her lip. Once again he was threatening to go too far. Tearing up some notes was one thing. Tampering with her electronics was another.

With a reluctant growl, he handed her back her things.

"Whatever," he said dismissively. "Do your thing. But just stay out of my way, okay?" He turned, running fingers through his thick hair and looking for his surf-board.

She quickly stashed her things away in her front pockets again, watching him anxiously. This seemed a lot like disaster in the making. He now knew who she was, so she couldn't very well follow him. If he found out she was questioning his neighbors, she wasn't sure what he would do, but she knew it wouldn't be pretty.

So she was stuck. Kelly couldn't do anything surrepti-tiously. Any new research would have to be done right out in the open and to his face. And for that she needed to have a civil relationship with him. That didn't seem to be in the cards, the way things were working out.

Without looking her way again, he began to stride off through the sand, his board under his arm.

She watched him go for a moment, watched the fog begin to swallow him up, her heart sinking. This couldn't be all there was. This couldn't be the end of her research. She might never know the truth now. Was he the prince or wasn't he? She had to find out. Gathering herself together, she ran after him.

"Wait!" she called. "Joe, wait a minute. I...I'll tell you everything."

He kept walking.

"Wait."

She caught up with him and managed to get him to glance at her again. "Have you ever heard of a little island country named Ambria?" she asked, searching his eyes for his reaction to her words.

He stopped in his tracks and turned, looking at her. And then he went very still. Everything about him seemed to be poised and waiting, like a cat in the jungle, preparing to strike.

"Ambria," he said slowly. Then he nodded, his eyes hooded. "Sure. I've heard of the place. What about it?"

There was something there. He'd reacted. She couldn't tell much, but there was a thread of interest in his gaze. Should she tell him what she thought she knew? She was trembling on the brink, but held back. The time wasn't right.

"Nothing," she said quickly, flushing and looking away to hide it. "I just…I'm Ambrian. Or I should say, my parents were. And I work for the Ambrian News Agency in Ohio."

He was searching her eyes, his own dark and clouded. "So?"

"I saw that article about the returning heroes six months ago where you were one of the soldiers featured."

He nodded, waiting.

"And…well, I got some information…. I'm following a lead that you might be Ambrian yourself. I'd like to talk to you about it and…"

He frowned. "Sorry." He turned from her again. "I'm not Ambrian. I'm American. You've got the wrong guy."

No. She didn't believe that. She'd seen the flicker behind his eyes.

"Wait," she said, hurrying after him again. "I really need your help."

She paused, realizing there was absolutely no reason

he should want to help her. She had to add something, something that would give him an excuse to get
involved.

"You see, what I'm doing is researching people who
were forced to leave Ambria by the revolution twenty-
five years ago. A lot of people were killed. A lot of the
royal family was killed."

He looked cynical. "Well, there you go. I wasn't
killed. And neither was my mother."

Kelly glanced up in surprise. "Who was your
mother?"

If he had a mother—a real mother—that could
change everything. Her entire investigation was riding
on a theory snatched out of thin air. At least that was
what they'd told her at headquarters.

Her mouth felt very dry. What if she'd come all the
way out here for nothing? Could she stand the ribbing
she would take when she went back to her office? Could
she hold her head up in meetings, or would she know
they were always thinking, *Don't pay any attention to
Kelly. She's the one who went on that wild-goose chase
after a lost prince who turned out to be not lost and not
a prince. Crazy woman.*

She cringed inside. But only for a moment.

Backbone, Kelly, she told herself silently. *Don't give
up without a fight.*

Holding her head high, she went back into attack
mode.

"Who was your mother?" she asked again, this
time almost accusingly, as though she was sure he was
making it up.

His mouth twisted and he looked at her as though he was beginning to wonder the same thing herself. "You know, I don't get it. What does this have to do with anything? It's all ancient history."

"Exactly. That's why I'm researching it. I'm trying to illuminate that ancient history and get some people reconnected with the background they've lost."

Meaning you, mister!

He was shaking his head. "I don't need any lost family. Family isn't really that important to me. It hasn't done me all that much good so far."

"But—"

Joe turned on her angrily. "Leave me alone, Kelly Vrosis. This is an important day for me and you've already wasted too much of it. Stay out of my way. I've got no time for this."

"Wow," she said, controlling herself, but letting her growing anger show. "And here I thought you were a good guy. The article I read made you sound like a hero."

He stared at her, his face dark and moody. "I'm no hero, Kelly. Believe me." He worked the muscles in his shoulders and grimaced painfully. "But I'm not a villain, either. As long as I'm not provoked."

"Oh, brother." She gave him a scathing look. "You can't call someone who's never been tempted a saint, can you?"

He studied her, his eyes cold. "I'm not really interested in your philosophy of life. And I still don't know who sent you here."

"I came on my own," she insisted.

He stared at her, then slowly shook his head. "I don't believe that."

He was striding off again, but this time she stayed where she was, blinking back the tears that threatened. There was no doubt about it, no tiny glimmer of hope. He'd closed the door. This investigation was over. There wasn't much more she could do.

CHAPTER THREE

JOE GLANCED AT his watch. It looked as if he still had a couple of hours to kill before heading to the airport. He knew he should be home preparing the place for the arrival of his little girl, and preparing his own psyche for how he was going to deal with her, but he was too rattled, too restless to stay in one place for long. He turned into his favorite coffee bar a couple blocks from his house and got into the line at the counter.

Yeah, coffee. Just the thing to settle his jangled nerves. What was he thinking? A good stiff shot of whiskey would have been better.

But he wasn't going to be drinking the hard stuff anymore, not while he had his daughter living with him. Everything was going to be different.

It had been hard enough just getting her here. Angie's mother, Coreline, had been against their marriage from the beginning, and she'd done all she could to keep Joe from bringing his baby home after Angie died. He'd been prepared, now that he was mostly healed, to go to the Philippines and fight for custody, but word had come suddenly that Coreline had died, and that baby

Mei would be sent to him right away, along with her nanny.

Thank God for the nanny! Without her, Joe would be in a panic right now. But luckily, she would stay for six months to help him adjust. In the meantime, he would make arrangements for the future.

His baby was coming to be with him. It was all he could think about.

The only thing that had threatened to distract him had been his strange encounter with Kelly Vrosis earlier that morning. Hopefully, his demeanor had discouraged her enough that he wouldn't see her again.

He took his drink from the counter and turned, sweeping his gaze through the crowded café, and there she was, sitting in the shadowy back corner. She'd cleaned up pretty well. Instead of the baggy clothes, she was wearing a snug yellow tank top and dark green cropped pants with tiny pink lizards embroidered all over them. His own crisp button-up shirt and nicely creased slacks added to the contrast of the way they had both looked that morning.

As his gaze met hers, she smiled and raised her hand in a friendly salute.

"Hi," she said as he came closer. Her smile looked a little shaky, but determined.

He grimaced and went over to her table, slumping down into the seat across from her.

"What are you having?" she asked, just to be polite. "A nice latte?"

He held up his cardboard cup. "A Kona blend, black. Extra bold."

She raised her eyebrows. "I should have known."

He didn't smile. "You're doing it again," he said wearily.

She looked as innocent as possible, under the circumstances. "Doing what?"

"Following me."

She pretended shock. "Of all the egos in the world! I was here first."

He gave her a look. "Come on, you know you are."

"Hey, I'm allowed to inhabit all the public spaces you inhabit until you get a court order to stop me."

He groaned. "Is it really going to take that?"

She stared at him frankly, pretending to be all confidence, but inside she was trembling. She'd almost given up a bit earlier, but it hadn't taken long to talk herself into giving it another try. Now here she was, trying hard, but it seemed he still wasn't buying.

"Kelly, don't make me get tough on you."

Was that a threat? She supposed it was, but she was ready to let that go as long as she had a chance to turn his mind around. She leaned forward earnestly. "You know how you could take care of this? Make it all go away like magic?"

He looked skeptical. "Maybe I could have you kidnapped and dropped off on an uninhabited South Pacific island," he suggested.

"No. All you have to do is sit down for an interview and let me ask you a few questions."

That hard line was back around his mouth and dark clouds filled his blue eyes. "So you *are* a writer."

"No, I'm not." She was aching with the need to find

a way to convince him. "I'm not interested in writing about you. I *wouldn't* write about you. I know it would be dangerous for you if I did, and I would never do anything to hurt you."

He studied her, uncertain what the hell she was talking about. She was pretty and utterly appealing, and he wasn't used to being mean to pretty girls. But did he have any choice? He needed to be rid of her.

"Listen, I came all the way from Ohio to find you. Let me talk to you for, say…one hour," she suggested quickly. "Just one."

He frowned at her suspiciously. "What about? What is it that you want to know?"

She brightened. "About you. About where you come from. Your background."

He shook his head. This didn't make any sense at all. "Why? What do you care about those things? I thought you were finding places for refugees from your island to go or something. What does all that have to do with me?"

"Because I think…" She took a deep breath. "Because there's plenty of evidence that you might be…"

"What?"

She coughed roughly and he resisted the urge to give her a good pat on the back. When she stopped, she still looked as though she didn't know what to say to him.

"What could it be?" he said, half teasing, half sarcastic. "Maybe Elvis's love child?"

"No." She licked her dry lips and forced herself onward. "Have you…have you ever heard of…the lost royals of Ambria?"

That damn island again. This was the second time she'd mentioned Ambria and she was the second person this week to bring up that little country. What the heck was going on? He stared at her for a long moment, then shrugged. "What about them?"

"I think you're one of them."

His brows came together for a second. "No kidding? Which one?" he added, though he didn't really know a thing about any of them, not even their names.

She took a deep breath. "I don't know that for sure. But I think Prince Cassius would be the right age."

Joe shook his head, an incredulous look on his face. "I want to understand this. You came to California just so you could follow me around and decide if you thought I was this prince?"

"Yes."

"Do you know how nutty that sounds?"

"Yes, I know exactly how nutty it sounds. Everyone I know has been telling me that ever since I got the idea."

He stared at her for a few seconds longer, and then he threw back his head and laughed aloud. "You're insane," he said, still laughing.

"No. I'm serious."

He shook his head again, rising and grabbing his cup. "I should have known better than to stop and talk to you," he muttered as he turned to go. Looking back, he laughed again.

"Now that I know you're unstable, I feel vindicated in not wanting to have anything to do with you and your crazy theories." He raised a hand in warning. "Stay out of my way, Kelly Vrosis. I mean it. Don't waste any more of my time."

She sat very still as she watched him walk away, and the realization hit her hard: he didn't know.

How amazing was that? If he really was one of the princes, he didn't know about it. It seemed almost unbelievable, and yet, somehow it fit with the way he'd been living his life. No one would have thought he was a prince.

No one but her.

She'd lived sith the story of the lost royals for months now. Twenty-five years ago, the mysterious little country of Ambria had been invaded by the Granvilli clan. The king and queen were killed, the castle was burned and the royal children—five sons and two daughters—had disappeared. For years it was assumed they had been murdered, too. But lately a new theory had surfaced. What if some of them had been spirited away and hidden all these years? What if the lost royal children of Ambria still existed?

That was the question that had filled her ever since she'd read about them. And once she saw the pictures of Joe in the magazine article, she'd been sure he was one of them.

And was she right? Could this ex-Army Ranger, this California surfer boy, really be one of the lost royals of Ambria? Could he really be a prince? He didn't act like it. But then, if he hadn't been raised to know how a prince was supposed to act, why would he?

Despite all that, the more she saw of him, the more confident she was in her instincts. The DeAngelis family that had ruled Ambria for over five hundred years had the reputation of being the most attractive royals ever. Her opinion? He fit right in.

"Mr. Tanner? This is Gayle Hannon at the customer service desk at the airport. There's been some sort of mix-up. A little girl has arrived designated for your reception, but—"

Joe gripped the receiver tightly. "She's here already? She wasn't supposed to arrive until tonight."

"As I say, there's been a mix-up. She was diverted to a different flight, and it seems the required child caretaker has disappeared. She's..." The woman's voice deepened with new emotion. "Mr. Tanner, she's all alone. Poor little thing. I think you had better come quickly."

"She's hardly more than one year old," he said, stunned. How had she ended up arriving alone on an international flight? "I'll be right there."

All alone. The words echoed in his mind as he searched for his keys and dashed for his car. This wasn't good. He had to get there, fast.

Kelly was out on the sidewalk in front of Joe's house, waiting for him. She'd spent the last few minutes giving herself a pep talk, and she was ready to hang tough this time. As he started his car out, she bent forward and knocked on the half-open passenger side window.

"Joe, listen. I've really got to talk to you. There is something you should know."

He looked at her blankly. "Huh?" he said. "What?"

She hesitated, sensing an opening. "Where are you going?"

"The airport," he said distractedly.

"Can I come with you? I just need to…"

He shook his head, not even listening. "Whatever," he muttered, pulling on his seat belt.

"Oh."

She took that as pure encouragement. Reaching out, she tugged on the door handle. Miraculously, it sprang right open and she jumped in.

"Great."

"Hey." He glared at her, finally seeming to realize who she was and why she was sitting beside him in his car. "Listen, I don't have time for this."

She smiled. "Okay," she said agreeably. "Let's go then."

He hesitated only a moment, then shook his head and swore. "What the hell." He grunted, stepping on the accelerator. "Hang on and keep quiet," he told her firmly. "I'm in a hurry."

She did as he said. He took the city streets too fast and then turned onto the freeway. Once he'd settled into a place in the flow of traffic, she turned and smiled brightly at him.

"So, the airport?" she said. "Are you meeting someone?"

He didn't even glance her way. "Yeah," he said, concentrating on his driving. Then he shook his head and muttered, "She's all alone in the middle of the airport and she's hardly more than one year old."

Kelly waited for a moment, and when he didn't elaborate, she asked, "Who is?"

He glanced at her sideways. "My little girl."

Kelly's jaw dropped. In all her time researching Joe Tanner, she'd never seen a shred of evidence that he had a child.

"Your little girl? What's her name?"

"Mei. Her mother named her. I wasn't there to help with it." He swore softly, shaking his head. "I was never there. Damn it. Some husband, huh?"

This was all news to Kelly. "You're married?" she asked, stunned.

He took in a deep breath and let it out. "I was married. Angie died in a firefight in the Luzon jungle a year ago. And now I'm finally going to meet our baby."

Kelly sat staring out at the landscape as they raced along. The enormity of what she'd thrown herself into finally registered, and it was like hitting a brick wall. She thought she knew so much, and now to find out she knew so little... Had she made a terrible mistake? All those months of researching this man and she didn't have a clue. He'd been married and had a baby? Stunning.

What else didn't she know? If she was so clueless about so much, could she possibly be right about his royal background? It didn't seem very likely at the moment. Heat filled her cheeks and she scrunched down in the seat, wishing she was somewhere else.

Traffic slowed to a crawl. Joe drummed his fingers on the steering wheel, mumbling to himself and looking pained. "What am I going to do with her?"

Kelly sat up straighter. He was obviously talking about his daughter. Why did he sound so lost, so troubled?

"Didn't you have a plan when you sent for her?" she asked.

He raised a hand and gestured in frustration. "There was supposed to be a nursemaid with her. Someone who knows her and can help take care of her."

There was anger in his voice, but also so much more. Kelly heard anxiety she would never have expected from such a strong personality. He'd obviously come up against something he didn't really understand, something he wasn't sure he could deal with. Despite everything, her heart went out to him.

"What happened?" she asked.

He shook his head. "I don't know. They called and said Mei had come in early and she was all alone." He turned and glanced at Kelly, and swore softly, obviously regretting that he'd let her into the car in a distracted moment.

"Why are you here?" he demanded, looking very annoyed. "This has nothing to do with you. And if you think you're going to write about this… Listen, I'm going to drop you off at a pay phone as soon as we get off this freeway."

"No." All thoughts of disappearing from the scene had flown right out of her mind. His dilemma had touched her. She wanted to help. "I swear to God, Joe, I will not write anything about you and your baby. I'm not a journalist. I'm not a writer." She took a deep breath. "And I'm coming with you."

"The hell you are!"

"Joe, don't you see? You need help. You can't handle a baby all by yourself."

"Sure I can. I bought a car seat." He nodded toward the back, and she turned and saw a state-of-the-art monstrosity sitting there, ready to go. Evidently he was ready to buy anything necessary for his child and pay for the best. That should be a good sign, she supposed. Still, he didn't seem to understand what taking care of a young child entailed.

"By handling a baby, I mean more than just putting her body someplace and telling her everything is okay." Kelly bit her lip and then appealed to his common sense. "She's going to be scared. You'll be driving. She'll need more attention than you can give her on the ride home. Face it. You're going to need help."

Kelly took his sullen silence to mean he saw her point, and she breathed in relief. As she studied his profile, her confidence began to creep back. Maybe she hadn't been so wrong about everything, after all. He was so handsome. Handsome and quite royal looking, if she did say so herself.

Joe spotted Mei as soon as he walked into the building. Just seeing her hit him like a thunderbolt.

She was sitting on a chair behind the airline check-in counter, her little legs out straight, her feet in their white socks and black Mary Janes barely reaching the edge. Her dark hair was cut off at ear length, with a thick fringe of bangs that almost covered her almond-shaped eyes. His heart flipped in his chest and suddenly he was out of breath.

Once he'd caught sight of her, he didn't see anything else. The rest of the world faded into a bothersome mist. There were people talking all around him, but he didn't hear a thing. She sat there as though there was a spotlight shining down on her, and he went straight for her.

Joe stopped in front of her, and for a moment he couldn't speak. His heart was full. He hadn't expected this. He was always the tough guy, the one who didn't get caught up in emotions. But from the moment he'd seen this little girl, he knew he was in love. She was so gorgeous, so adorable, he could hardly stand it.

"Mei?" he said at last, his voice rough.

She looked up and stared into his eyes, her little round face expressionless.

"Hi, Mei," he said. "I'm…I'm your daddy."

There was no change, no response. For a second, he wondered if she hadn't heard him.

"I'm taking you home," Joe said. His voice broke on that last word.

Gazing up at him, she shook her head. "No," she said, looking worried.

He stared at her, hardly hearing her or noticing her mood. For so long she'd been a dream in his heart, and now she was here.

And suddenly, the past came flooding in on him. He saw his beautiful Angie again, saw her trembling smile. Saw the love in her eyes as she greeted him, the delight as she told him of the new baby he'd never seen, the fear as their hiding place was discovered by the rebels…the gunfire… Saw the peace and acceptance on her lovely face as she died in his arms. He remembered the agonizing cry ripped from his chest as he'd realized he'd lost her forever, remembered the gut-wrenching fury as he'd taken off through the jungle after her murderers. Felt again the searing pain as their bullets hit his flesh, the aching frustration as he fell to the ground, helpless.

It all came back in a flash, and Joe tried to shake it away just as quickly. He couldn't let this precious child, this gift of love between him and Angie, be hurt by the ugly past.

Still, the past was what it was. He couldn't change it. It had made him into the bitter recluse he was today. But he wasn't going to inflict that on the child. Looking at her now, he knew he was going to do everything he could for her in every way. His heart seemed to swell in his chest. She would be his life from now on. But why did it hurt so much?

"For you, Angie," he murmured softly, his voice choking, his vision blurring with tears.

Kelly looked at Joe in surprise. All she'd seen so far was his tough side, the sarcasm, the arrogance, the disdain. She'd never dreamed such a very small girl could bring a man like this to tears.

Kelly had come in right behind him, but was trying to stay to the side and out of the way. She didn't want to intrude, didn't want to push in where she didn't belong, but he was just standing there, paralyzed with emotion. If she didn't do something, he was going to scare the poor kid to death. There was really no choice. She stepped forward.

"Hi, sweetie," she said with a cheery smile, bending down. "My name's Kelly. I'm your daddy's friend. I'm going to help take you home. Okay?"

The huge dark eyes stared at her solemnly. For a moment, Kelly thought there would be no response. The child's gaze seemed flat, emotionless. Her little features didn't move at all.

Kelly glanced at Joe for guidance, but the look on his face told her he wouldn't even hear her right now.

"Mei?" Kelly said, smiling hopefully. "You want to come with me?"

As though a veil was lifted, Mei's eyes lit with interest and her little head nodded.

Flooded with relief, Kelly put out her arms and Mei went to her willingly, then clung to her. And that was that. Mei seemed to think she belonged with Kelly. No room for other options.

They waited for a required interview with a supervisor, then Joe began to make his way through the paperwork, while Kelly tried to keep the baby entertained as best she could. The bustle of people all around them helped. Whenever Mei felt anxious, Kelly was there to soothe away her fears. At the same time she kept one ear open to the questions Joe was answering, hoping to glean something that would help with her identification. She didn't get much there, but she did hear the name Angie repeated often enough to realize that had to be Mei's mother, and Joe's wife. One look at his face was all she needed to understand the tragedy involved in his losing her.

Kelly noticed that Joe was very carefully avoiding

glancing at Mei. She thought she knew why. He was protecting himself, just getting through the bureaucratic formalities with all due speed. This child had power over him, and he had to wait until they were out of here before he could begin learning how to deal with it.

They were almost done when Joe visibly steeled himself and turned to smile at his daughter.

"Okay, Mei," he said, holding out his arms. "Why don't you let me carry you for awhile?"

The baby shrank away, and as his hands touched her, she let out a shriek that could probably be heard all the way back to Manila. Joe jerked back, his face like stone. He glanced at Kelly, who was at a loss as to how to fix this situation, and then he turned and walked back to the airline counter, where he had a bit more business to complete.

Kelly held Mei closely, knowing this was not good, and feeling a surge of compassion for Joe that almost brought her to tears. But what could she do?

Once all the paperwork was done and they were heading for the parking lot, little Mei's arms went around Kelly's neck and she snuggled in tightly. But whenever Joe turned to look at her, she stiffened, and Kelly began to realize there might be more problems ahead than he had ever anticipated.

CHAPTER FOUR

JOE WAS SILENT on the drive home from the airport.
He was the sort of man who liked to be in command of
every situation, understanding what was needed, hitting all the bases. The problem was, right now he didn't
have a clue. He felt like a swimmer who couldn't touch
bottom and had lost sight of the beach. What was he
supposed to do now?

The idea of a baby daughter had seemed vaguely
pleasant. A little girl to call his own. A miniature ver-
sion of Angie, maybe—sweet, pretty, a blessing in his
life. She was his child and his responsibility.

He'd pictured a friendly meeting at the airport. The
nanny would be in charge. After all, he'd been told the
woman had been taking care of Mei ever since she was
born. He would drive them home, and that would be
that. A child in his life—but a child with a caretaker,
someone who knew what she was doing.

That was the plan. Reality had caught him unprepared and hit him like a blow to the gut.

No nanny. No caretaker. No safety net.

That wasn't going to work. He didn't know the first

thing about taking care of a kid this age. Or any age, really.

But even worse had been his own emotional reaction to seeing little Mei in the flesh for the first time. He hadn't expected to have the pain flood in that way. His stomach turned again just thinking about it. If he'd known that was going to happen…

Traffic was light, but his headlights bounced against the fog and he had to pay close attention, peering into the darkness as though he might find some answers there. Kelly was sitting next to Mei in the back, talking to her softly, helping her play with a toy attached to the car seat.

He listened for a moment, craning to hear, as though she were speaking in a foreign language he didn't understand. And he didn't. What was he doing here? What was he going to do with this child?

"Did you find out what happened to the nanny?" Kelly asked him as he turned off the freeway and stopped at a red light.

He hesitated, reluctant to tell her anything. She shouldn't even be here. Still, if she wasn't, he would be in even bigger trouble. He supposed he owed her a bit of civility, if nothing else.

"They said she was seen with Mei right up until they went through customs here at the airport, and then she disappeared." He shook his head in disbelief. "They found her sitting there in one of those plastic chairs. She had a tag around her neck with her papers and my name and all that. They gave me the address the nanny used as a contact point, but something tells me that's going to be useless."

He glanced in the rearview mirror. He couldn't see Mei, but that was okay. Right now he didn't want to.

"They said it happens all the time. She'll probably blend right into the immigrant community and it will be hard to ever find her."

Kelly nodded. "That's what I was afraid of."

He frowned and didn't speak again as he turned onto his street and pulled into the driveway.

"You're lucky," Kelly said softly. "She's asleep. I'll bet you can carry her in without waking her."

"Good."

"Do you have a bed for her?"

He turned off the engine and looked back. "Of course I have a bed for her. I've got a whole room ready."

"Oh. Good."

He got out and held the rear door open. He was still avoiding taking a look at Mei. Instead, he studied Kelly, noting that she'd pulled her curly blonde hair back and tied it with a band, though strands were escaping and making a halo effect around her face. She had a sweet, pretty face. She looked nice. His baby needed somebody nice. What if he asked her to stay and…

Grimacing, he turned and looked into the fog that surrounded his house. What was he thinking? He didn't need a woman like this hanging around, distracting him from the work he had to do creating a family for this baby. He should tell Kelly to take a hike. She had no business being here with them. He didn't know her. And she was all wrong for this job. The last thing he wanted for a nanny was a woman this appealing to the senses. She had to go.

Still, the thought of being alone with Mei struck a certain level of terror in his heart. He needed help. Who was he going to get to come at this time of night?

"What are you going to do?" Kelly asked softly, standing in front of him.

He shrugged. "Try to hire a nanny, I guess," he said gruffly.

"You won't be able to do that until morning."

He nodded.

"I'll stay," she said. It was less an offer than a firm statement of intent.

"You?" He looked at her with a scowl. Suspicions flooded back. He may have just been considering asking her to stay, but why was she offering? "Why would you do that? You're not going to get a story out of me."

She threw up her hands in exasperation. "I told you, I'm not looking for a story. I'm not a writer."

She'd said that again and again. But if she wasn't trying to get a story, what was her angle? Everybody had one.

"Then what *do* you want, Kelly?" he asked.

She gazed up into his troubled eyes. She wasn't sure why this was all so upsetting to him, but she could see that it was. He was fairly bristling with tension. Was it just that he didn't know how to take care of a baby and was nervous about it?

No, she was pretty sure it was something more. Something deeper and more painful. Everything in her yearned to help him, human to human. This had nothing to do with her quest for his real identity.

"What I want is to help you. To help the baby."

She saw the doubt in his face, and reached out and touched his arm. "Seriously, Joe. Right now that's all I care about."

He searched her eyes. "I'm telling you straight out, I don't trust you," he said gruffly. "But at the moment, I feel I don't really have a choice. With the nanny gone..." He shrugged, not needing to complete the sentence. His blue eyes were clouded. "You've seen the way Mei reacts to me."

Kelly bit her lip and nodded. She'd been wondering if he'd really noticed, wondering if that was what was hurting him. An unexpected feeling of tenderness toward him flooded her. There was no way she was going to leave him alone with his baby until...well, she didn't know. But not yet.

He looked at her and saw the softening in her face. Suddenly he was breathless. That halo effect her hair had was working again. She looked like an angel.

He didn't want to need her. He wanted to pick up his little girl and carry her into the house and live happily ever after, without Kelly Vrosis being involved in any way. But that wasn't going to happen.

He didn't want to need this woman, but he did.

"Do you have any real experience?" he asked, as though interviewing her for the job. "Any children?"

She shook her head. "I'm not married," she told him. "But I do have two brothers, and they both have kids. I've spent plenty of time caring for my nieces and nephews. I'll be okay."

He stared at her a moment longer, then shrugged.

"You want to bring in her stuff?" he asked shortly, nodding toward the baggage that had come across the Pacific with Mei as he leaned in to unbuckle the baby seat from the car.

"Sure," Kelly said, working hard on looking non-threatening, efficient and cheerful as she gathered the things together. "Lead the way."

He took her through a nice, ordinary living room, down a hallway and into an enchanting little girl's paradise. Kelly gazed around in wonder. The carpet was like walking on marshmallows and it was shiny clean. A beautiful wooden crib stood against one wall, an elaborate changing table beside it. A large, overstuffed recliner sat in one corner. The closet doors opened to reveal exquisitely organized baby clothes on shelves and hangers, along with row upon row of adorable toys.

"Joe, this is perfect. I can't believe you did this on your own."

"I didn't. I hired a consultant to help me."

She almost laughed at the thought. "A consultant?"

"From Dory's Baby Boutique in the village. The woman who runs it knows someone who does these things, and she set me up with a meeting." He put the car seat down and picked up a business card left on top of the changing table. "Sonja Smith, Baby Decorator," he read.

Kelly looked around the room in admiration, her gaze

caught by the framed pictures of cartoon elephants in tutus and walruses in tights. "She does a great job."

Standing in the middle of the room, looming over a sleeping Mei in her car seat, he raised one dark eyebrow and looked at Kelly speculatively. "Maybe you know her?"

She glanced at him in surprise. "No. Why would I know her?"

He shrugged again. "She was sort of pushing me about this whole Ambrian thing, too."

Kelly's eyes widened and her heart lurched in her chest. "What?"

"So you thought you were my first?" he said, showing amusement at her reaction.

Kelly's imagination began to churn out crisis scenarios like ravioli out of a pasta machine, but she held back. She knew better than to pursue it now. The focus had to be on Mei.

Joe moved the car seat closer to the bed, obviously wondering how he was going to make the transfer to the crib without waking his little girl. Kelly started to give him some suggestions, but he did a great job on his own, laying her gently on the mattress. Kelly pulled a soft blanket over her and they both stood looking down at her.

"She's adorable," Kelly said softly.

He closed his eyes and leaned on the rail, his knuckles white. His reaction worried her.

"Joe, what is it?"

He turned toward her, his eyes dark and haunted. He stared at her for a moment, then shook his head.

"Nothing," he said gruffly. "But listen, I really appreciate that you offered to stay. I'm going to need the help."

"Of course you are."

And then she realized he didn't only mean with the care and feeding of a small girl. There was something else tearing him apart. For a man like this, one usually so strong and so confident, to admit he needed help was a big step. She wasn't even thinking about the whole prince thing any longer. She was thinking about the man standing here, looking so lost, racked with some kind of pain that she couldn't begin to analyze.

"I'll sleep right here in the room," Kelly said quickly.

He looked around. "There's no bed."

"The chair reclines. With a pillow and a blanket, I'll be fine."

He frowned. "You won't be comfortable there."

"Sure I will. And I want to be right here in case she wakes up. She'll be scared. She'll need someone at least a little bit familiar."

He moved restlessly, then looked at Kelly sideways. "Okay. I don't have any women's clothes hanging around, but I can give you a T-shirt to sleep in."

She smiled at him. Despite everything, he looked very appealing with his hair tousled and falling over his forehead, and his eyes heavy and sleepy and his mouth so wide and inviting....

Whoa. She pulled herself up short. Where the heck did she think she was going with that thought?

"Uh...a T-shirt would be perfect," she said quickly, her cheeks heating as she turned away.

"Okay."

He didn't seem to notice her embarrassment. Without another word, he left the room.

She let her breath out slowly, fanning her cheeks. She had to remember who he was. Or at least, who she thought he was. She wasn't getting very far on that project—but there would be time. Hopefully.

Joe returned with pillows, a comforter and a bright blue T-shirt that looked big enough to be a small dress on Kelly. She began to set up the chair for sleeping.

He frowned, watching her. "I should be the one to do that. I should sleep in here tonight."

"No," she said firmly. "If she wakes up, you might scare her."

For just a moment, he looked stricken, and Kelly regretted her quick words.

"This is ridiculous," he said, his voice gravelly with emotion. "She's my baby. I've got to find a way..."

"Joe." Kelly felt the ache in him and could hardly stand it. Reaching out, she took his hand, as though to convey by touch what her words couldn't really express. "Joe, it's not time yet. Don't you see? She's probably been raised by only women so far, and to her, you're big and male and scary. She's not sure what to do with you yet. You've barely met at this point. You've got to give her a little time."

"Time," he echoed softly, staring down at Kelly, his gaze hooded. He didn't seem receptive, but he wasn't pulling away from her grip on his hand.

"Yes. She's clueless right now. The one person she depended on, the nanny, deserted her. Mei doesn't know what you might do. Let her get to know you gradually."

"You're probably right." He said it reluctantly, but turned the tables so that he was holding *her* hand, and slowly raised it to his lips, kissing her fingers softly.

Kelly held her breath. She hadn't expected anything like that. But he didn't look into her eyes as he did it, and he didn't say anything more, so when he dropped her hand again, she felt almost as though he'd done it anonymously. Or maybe it was a sort of thank-you for her assistance.

Maybe she'd imagined the whole thing. Or maybe he was just distracted. He was definitely confusing her.

"Uh…thanks, Kelly," Joe said as he turned to go. "Thanks for staying."

She sent a radiant smile his way. "No problem. See you in the morning."

He stared back at her for a long moment, then nodded and left the room.

She shivered. What was it about haunted handsome men that was so compelling?

Sighing, she turned back to the crib. Looking down at the sleeping child, she wanted to brush the hair off her forehead, but was afraid that would waken her. What a beautiful little girl!

"Well," Kelly murmured to herself, "what have you gotten yourself involved in now?"

And then she remembered what he'd said about the designer and Ambria. Alarm bells were still ringing in her head over that one. She wanted to know more. She *had* to know more. But right now he wasn't going to be interested in anything that had to do with the obscure island nation, not until things were a bit more settled in his life.

Kelly only hoped they had the time to wait.

Sleeping in a recliner quickly lost its charm, but she got in a few dozing sessions before Mei stirred. When she heard her, she got up quickly and went to the crib, talking to the baby softly and patting her back until she fell asleep again.

By then Kelly was wide awake and thinking about what she might need the next time Mei woke up. Moving quietly, she opened the door and went silently through the darkened house to the kitchen, to see what Joe had done with the baby bottles and other supplies they had brought from the airport.

The layout of the house was simple, but she'd never been there before, so she was feeling her way when a movement caught her eye, stopping her cold. Someone was on the deck. She could see a dark form through the French doors. Her heart jumped into her throat and she shrank back against the wall, where she wouldn't be seen.

But even as she did so, she realized it had to be Joe. Kelly breathed a sigh of relief and went to the doors. Yes, there he was, leaning on the railing and gazing out toward the ocean—and looking like a man going through hell. Compassion flooded her and she sighed, wishing she knew what she could do to help him.

* * *

Joe tried to pull himself together. "Hell" had been watching the woman he loved die. This wasn't fun, but it was a piece of cake compared to that.

Not to say that it was easy. Seeing Mei reminded him of losing Angie, and that had opened up the past in a bad way. He had earned his agony, but he didn't have a right to take it out on anyone else. He'd gone through a lot a year ago. He'd hated life for awhile, hated his fate, his luck and everything else he could think of. But that was over.

He thought he'd mostly taken care of this already, during all the hours of therapy in the veterans hospital, the long nights of soul searching. He'd finally come to terms with what had happened, and said goodbye to Angie. Hadn't he?

But that was before he'd seen Mei.

That same old deadly agony was lurking. If he let it all flood back over him, he was going to drown. He couldn't go through that again. His eyes were stinging, and suddenly he realized why. Tears. What the hell? He never cried. This was ridiculous. Now, twice in one night… Leaning against the railing, he swore at himself, softly and obscenely. No more tears.

His head jerked up as he heard the door to the deck open. There Kelly stood, lighting up the gloom with her wild golden hair. How could this be hell if he had his own personal angel?

"Hi," she said. "You can't sleep, either?"

He turned slowly to face her, and she peered at him. It was too dark for her to see if his expression was welcoming, or if he wished she'd just go away. That wouldn't be so unusual. He usually seemed to want her gone.

But she wasn't going to go. She had a feeling he was out here brooding, and she didn't think that was a good thing.

"Are you okay?" she asked as she approached.

He didn't answer. He was dressed in jeans and a huge, baggy dark blue sweatshirt with a hood pulled up over his head, while she stood before him in nothing but his bright blue T-shirt. A cool breeze brought in a touch of chill, reminding her of her skimpy nightgown, and she hugged herself, giving thanks that the slip of a moon wasn't giving much light.

Looking up at him for a moment, she still couldn't read his eyes. In fact, she could barely make out the features of his face, hiding there in the shadows of his hoodie. Her heart was beginning to thump again. Why didn't he say anything? Was he angry? Did he think she was meddling? She couldn't tell and she was getting nervous.

She stepped past him and leaned on the rail next to him, looking out at what moonlight there was shimmering on the distant ocean. She could hear the waves, but couldn't see them. Too many houses blocked the view.

"I can tell you're upset," she said tentatively. "Do you want to talk about it?"

"Talk about it!" He coughed and cleared his throat. "You like guys who spill their guts, do you?"

Kelly was glad he'd finally spoken. Still, she could tell that something was bothering him. She could see it, feel it. And if talking it out could soften that sense of turmoil in him, it would be best to do it.

And not just for his sake. If he wasn't careful, his vibes were going to scare the baby. He needed to grapple with it, get rid of it, before he attempted to deal with the new little girl in his life. Kelly sighed, hardly believing what she was thinking. What made her so sure of these things, anyway? She didn't usually walk around claiming to have all the answers, and she knew very well she was groping in the dark as much as anyone.

But there was a child at stake here. For the sake of the baby, she had to do what she could.

"I know you don't really know me," she told him earnestly, "but that might make it easier. In a few days, I'll be gone and you'll never see me again." She gave him an apologetic smile. "Honest. I don't plan to stay in California any longer than that. So if you want to…I don't know…vent or something, feel free."

He looked at her and didn't know whether to laugh or hang his head. So this was what he'd come to—women volunteering to let him cry on their shoulders. How pathetic was that?

Well, he wasn't ready to open his heart to her, probably never would be. But he wouldn't mind another perspective on what he was torturing himself with at the moment. For some unknown reason, he felt as though he could talk to Kelly in ways he seldom did with other women.

Maybe, he thought cynically, it was the same quality in her that made Mei think she was a safe harbor in a scary world. Whatever it was, he supposed it wouldn't hurt to try.

"Okay, Kelly, you asked for it." He turned toward her. "Here's what I'm thinking." He hesitated, taking a deep breath before going on. "I'm thinking this whole thing was a very bad idea."

Just hearing that said out loud made him cringe inside.

She frowned at him, confused. "What was a bad idea?"

"To bring Mei here."

She gasped. "What are you talking about? She's your baby."

"Yeah." He turned and leaned on the railing. "But it was selfish. I was thinking about having an adorable little girl of my own, like she was a doll or something." He looked at her, despising himself a little. "A pet. A kitten."

"Oh, Joe."

"I know better, of course. She's a real human being." He shook his head. Thinking of Mei and her cute little face, he couldn't help but smile. "A beautiful, perfect little human being. And she…she deserves the best of everything."

Turning from Kelly, he began to pace the wooden deck, his hands shoved deep into his pockets. "I didn't think…I didn't realize… I can't really give her what she deserves. Maybe I should have left her with Angie's family. Maybe she would have been better off."

Kelly stepped forward and blocked his way, grabbing

handfuls of sweatshirt fabric at chest level to stop him in his tracks.

"No," she told him forcefully, her eyes blazing.

He stopped and looked down at her in surprise. "No?"

"No. You're wrong."

He bit back the grin that threatened to take over his face. She looked so fierce. And then it came to him—she really did care about this.

"What makes you so sure about that?" he asked her.

"Common sense." She tried to shake him with the grip she had on his sweatshirt. She didn't manage to move his body, but got her point across. "She's your responsibility."

He winced, his gaze traveling over the planes of Kelly's pretty face. She had good cheekbones and beautiful eyelashes. But her mouth was where his attention settled. Nice lips. White teeth. And a sexy pout that could start to get to him if he let it.

"You're right," he told her at last. "You're absolutely right." Then he added softly, "How'd you get to be so right about things?"

She released his shirt, pretty sure she'd convinced him, then lifted her chin and gazed into his eyes. He was so handsome and so troubled, and she wanted so badly to help him, but she couldn't resist teasing him a little.

"I'm an objective observer. You should take my advice on everything."

"Fat chance." He chucked her under the chin and

made a face. "You're the one who wants me to start chasing royal moonbeams, aren't you?"

She caught her breath, wanting to argue, wanting to tell him he was going to be surprised once she'd really explained things. But she stopped herself. It still wasn't time.

She needed more information before she jumped in with both feet. She wouldn't want to raise false hopes. She shivered, as much with that thought as with the cold.

"I'm no prince. Look at me." His voice took on a bitter edge. "My baby's even scared of me."

"That won't last. Give her time."

He nodded, a distant look in his eyes. "My head says you're right, but my heart..." He shrugged. "Like Shakespeare wrote, 'there's the rub.'"

She smiled. A man who quoted Shakespeare. "Where did you get so literary?" she asked him. "I didn't think you went to university."

"I didn't. I signed up for the army as soon as I graduated from high school. But I read a lot."

"In the army?" That didn't fit her preconception.

"Sure. Once you get deployed overseas you have a lot of downtime."

"I thought army guys usually filled that with wine, women and song."

He nodded. "Okay, you got me there. I did my share of blowing off steam. But that gets old pretty fast, and our base had a great library. Plus, the master sergeant was a real scholar, and he introduced me to what I should be reading."

Joe frowned when he saw her shivering. "You're cold."

She nodded. "I should go in."

"Here, this will take care of it."

In one swoop, he loosened the neck of his sweatshirt, then lifted the hem, capturing her under it. Before she knew what was happening, he'd pulled her in to join him.

"What are you doing?" she cried, shocked.

"Shhh." His arms came around her, holding her close, and he whispered next to her ear, "You're going to wake up the neighbors."

The thought of anyone seeing them this way sent her into giggles. "Joe, this is crazy."

Was he just close so that he could whisper to her, or was he snuggling in behind her ear?

"Warm enough?" he asked.

"Oh, yes. Definitely warm."

Though she had to admit *hot* might be a better word. The darkness and the fact that her face was half hidden in the neck of the shirt saved her from having him see how red her cheeks had turned. His skin was bare under the sweatshirt, and now she was pressed against his fantastic, muscular chest. If it hadn't been for her thick T-shirt...

It doesn't mean a thing, she warned herself, and knew that was right. But how could she resist the warmth and the wonderful smoothness of his rounded muscles against her face? She closed her eyes, just for a moment. His arms held her loosely, and since they were outside, wrapped in fabric, it was okay. She knew he was purposely trying to keep this nonthreatening, and she appreciated it. But no matter how casual he tried to make this, she was trapped in an enclosed space against his bare upper body. Her heart was beating like a drum and her head was feeling light. If she'd been a Victorian miss, she would be crying out for the smelling salts about now.

But she wasn't Victorian. She was up-to-date and full of contemporary attitudes. Wasn't she? She'd had sex and provocative bodies and scandalous talk thrown at her by the media all her life. She could handle this. Never mind that her knees seemed to be buckling and her pulse was racing so fast she couldn't catch her breath. This was worth it. This was heavenly. It was a moment she would never forget.

And then she remembered that he was supposed to be a prince of Ambria. She had no right to trifle with him this way. That thought made her laugh again.

"Joe, let me go," she said, pushing away. "I've got to go in and check on Mei."

"And leave me out here all alone in this sweatshirt?"

"I think you'll be able to manage it." She wriggled free, then shook her head in mock despair as she looked at him. "I feel like I was highjacked by the moonlight bandit," she grumbled, straightening her T-shirt nightdress.

His grin was crooked. "Think of me as the prince of dreams," he said, and then his mouth twisted. "Bad dreams," he added cynically.

"Stop agonizing out here in the dark and go get some sleep," she advised as she turned to leave. "Mei is going to need you in the morning."

CHAPTER FIVE

KELLY SLEPT LATER than she'd planned, and when she opened her eyes, sunlight was streaming into the room. She turned her head and found a pair of gorgeous dark eyes considering her from the crib. Mei was standing at the railing, surveying the situation.

"Good morning, beautiful," Kelly said, stretching. "Did you have a good sleep?"

The cute little face didn't change, but the baby reached down to pick up a stuffed monkey that had been in her bed, and threw it over the nail as though it were a gift. Kelly laughed, but wondered how long she'd been awake, just standing there, looking around the unfamiliar room, wondering where she was and who was going to take care of her. Poor little thing.

Rising quickly, Kelly went to her. "I'll bet you need a change, don't you?"

She didn't wait for an answer, and Mei didn't resist, going willingly into her arms. Kelly held her for a moment, feeling the life that beat in her, feeling her sweetness. There was no way Joe was sending her back. No way at all.

* * *

Joe was waiting for them when they came into the kitchen. He had coffee brewed and cinnamon buns warmed and sitting on the table. He'd set two places and poured out two little glasses of orange juice. Kelly was carrying Mei and she smiled at how inviting everything looked. Including Joe, who'd made the effort to dress in fresh slacks and a baby-blue polo shirt just snug enough to show off his muscular chest and bulging biceps.

He caught her assessing look and smiled. She quickly glanced away, but in doing so, her gaze fell on where he'd tossed the big blue sweatshirt over the back of a chair. Memories of how it had felt inside that shirt the night before crashed in on her like a wave, and suddenly her cheeks were hot again. She glanced at him. His smile had turned into a full grin.

He was just too darn aware of things.

"Here's your baby," she said, presenting his child for inspection. "Isn't she beautiful in her little corduroy dress?"

"She is indeed," he said brightly, looking warmly at his child. "Good morning, Mei. Can you give me a smile today?"

Evidently not. His daughter shrank back, hiding her face in Kelly's hair and wrapping her chubby arms tightly around her neck.

Kelly sent Joe an anxious glance, wishing she knew what to do to make this better. His smile hadn't faded, though his eyes showed some strain. She approved of the effort he was making. He met her gaze and nodded cheerfully.

"New attitude," he told her.

"Oh. Good." She managed to smile back. "I guess."

"I'm going to take your advice and learn to roll with the punches."

"Did I advise that?" she murmured, gratified that he was at least thinking about what she'd said.

He moved into position so that Mei couldn't avoid looking at him.

"Tell me," he asked her, "what does a little girl your age like to eat?"

Mei scrunched up her face as though she'd just tasted spinach for the first time.

Kelly sighed, but decided to try ignoring the baby's reactions for awhile and hope they faded on their own. Chastising her would do no good. She was a little young for a heart-to-heart talk, so that pretty much left patience. Kelly just hoped she didn't run out of it.

"I know when my niece was this age, she was all about finger food. She loved cut up bananas and avocados, and for awhile she seemed to live on cheese cut up into little squares."

He nodded. "I'll have to make a store run. I'd pretty much counted on the nanny to be the expert in this sort of thing."

"We can wing it for now," Kelly assured him. "And for the moment, I'll bet she would like one of those yogurts I saw in the refrigerator."

"You think so?" He pulled one out and held it up. "How about it, Mei? Ready for some yummy yogurt?"

Her gaze was tracking the yogurt cup as though she

hadn't eaten in days, but when he moved close with it, she hid her face again.

"I guess you'll have to give it to her," he said drily. "She's pretty sure I'm the serpent with the apple at this point."

Mei went into the high chair willingly enough after Kelly let her toddle around on her little chubby legs for a few minutes, but she kept her eye on Joe, reacting when he came too close.

"Don't worry," Kelly told him, smiling as they sat down at the table and she began to feed Mei from her yogurt cup with a plastic spoon shaped like a dolphin. "She'll come around."

He smiled back, but it wasn't easy. They talked inconsequentially for a few moments. Mei ate her yogurt lustily, then played with some cheese Kelly cut up for her. Joe offered Mei a bite of cinnamon roll, but she shook her head and looked at him suspiciously.

"You've gotten over those doubts you had last night, haven't you?" Kelly asked at one point, needing reassurance.

"Sure," he said, dismissing it with a shrug. "Funny how the middle of the night makes everything look so impossible." He gave her a sideways smile. "And yet makes doing things like snuggling in a sweatshirt suddenly seem utterly rational."

"You dreamer," she murmured, holding back her smile and giving Mei her last bite of yogurt. Then Kelly looked at him sharply. "But you aren't still thinking of…" She couldn't finish that sentence without saying things she didn't want to say in front of the child.

He shrugged again. "I know what I have to do. I think I understand my responsibilities."

She frowned. She would have been happier if he'd sounded more enthusiastic, but she had to admit she understood. In the face of so much rejection, it was pretty hard to get very excited. She wanted to tell him not to worry, that surely things would get better soon. There was no way he could stand a lifetime like this—no one could. But he wouldn't have to.

And you know this…how? her inner voice mocked her.

Kelly wasn't sure about that, but knew it had to be true.

"Are you going to be calling an agency to find a new nanny?" It was sad to think of someone else coming in and taking over, but it had to be done. She couldn't stay forever.

"I already have."

"Already? You're fast."

"Well, I called and left a message on a machine. They weren't open yet. But I have no doubt we'll get someone out here by this afternoon at the latest."

"Well, there's no hurry," Kelly told him. "I'll stay until you get someone else."

His eyes darkened and he gazed at her for a moment as though trying to figure out what made her tick.

"Don't you have someplace you need to be?" he asked at last.

"Not at all. My week is wide open."

He looked as though he didn't get her at all. "So you really did come here to California just to find me?"

She nodded.

He shook his head as though she must be crazy. She braced herself for questions, but he didn't seem to want to deal with it yet. Rising from his place, he took his plate to the sink.

Watching him in profile, she was struck once again by how much he looked like a member of the royal family of Ambria. She was going to have to bring that up again soon. But in the meantime, there was another issue to deal with.

"Joe, tell me something," she said as he put the orange juice in the refrigerator. "This designer person who brought up Ambria…"

He turned to face her, then sank back into his chair at the table. "Sonja Smith? What about her?"

Kelly wasn't sure how to go about this delicately, so she just jumped in. "What exactly did she say to you?"

He thought for a second. "She didn't say anything much. She said that Dory at the Baby Boutique had told her she thought I might be from Ambria. That's all."

"Why did the Baby Boutique person think you were Ambrian?"

He shook his head. "I don't know. I went in a week ago and talked to her about needing some advice on stocking a baby's room, and she told me about Sonja and had her call me." He grimaced. "I don't know where she got the idea for the Ambrian connection. I never said anything to Dory about that. I'm sure Ambria never came up. In fact, the existence of Ambria hadn't entered my mind in…oh, I'd say a year or two. As far as countries go, it's not high on my list." He shrugged. "The point is, Ambria isn't a favorite of mine. And I have no idea why anyone would think I was interested."

"Hmm." Kelly gazed at him thoughtfully.

"Sonja came over, did a great job, and that was it. End of story."

"That's all?"

He made a face. "Well, not really. She wasn't just a designer decorator. Turns out she also tries to rustle up customers for tours she arranges. She works at a travel agency and was putting together a tour to Europe, including Ambria, in the summer. She said if I was interested I should give her a call. She thought I'd enjoy it."

Kelly didn't know what to think about that. It seemed a bit strange. Of course, there could be any number of reasons someone of Ambrian heritage might find his face appealing—and familiar, just as she had. It might be completely innocent, just a businesswoman trying to drum up sales for her tour.

On the other hand, it might be someone allied with the usurper Ambrian regime, the Granvillis. And from everything she'd learned lately, if the Granvillis were after you, you were in big trouble. Joe was taking all this lightly, but she was afraid he didn't know the background the way she did. If he had, he might have been more on guard.

That meant she'd better tell him soon. It was only fair to warn him. The fact that she knew he would scoff at her warnings didn't encourage her, but she knew it had to be done. And that somehow she was going to have to convince him.

"Well? Are you interested in the tour?"

He gave her an amused look, then rose to take the rest of the plates to the sink. "No. I've never had a yen to travel to a place like that. In fact, I've done enough foreign travel for awhile. I think I'll stay put."

She nodded. "Are you going to see her again?"

"Maybe. She might come by to meet Mei. I suggested it. I thought she might like to see what the child she did all this for looked like in the midst of it." He frowned, turning to face Kelly. "Listen, what's with the third degree? Does this somehow impinge upon your royal dreams?"

She shook her head. He was teasing her, but she wasn't in a teasing mood. Until she found out what this designer person was up to, she was going to be very uneasy. "Not a bit," she claimed cheerfully. Glancing up, she saw that he was looking at Mei, his face set and unhappy. It broke her heart, and she immediately had the urge to do something about it.

Rising and moving to stand close to him at the sink, she leaned in so she could speak softly and not be overheard by Mei. She'd been thinking about different schemes for getting the child to accept Joe. She could hardly stand to see the obvious pain in his face when his little girl rejected him.

"Here's a thought," Kelly said, very near his ear. "Why don't you just go over and sit by Mei and talk. Don't even talk to her at first, just near her. You could talk about your past with her mother. Maybe tell her how you met. Or anything else you can think of. Her name was Angie, right?"

He turned on her as though she'd suggested he sing an aria from La Bohème. "What? Why would I do any of that?"

Kelly blinked up at him, surprised at his vehemence. "Okay, if you don't want to do it directly, why don't you tell *me* about Angie in front of Mei. About where you met her, what your wedding was like, things like that."

His complete rejection of her idea was written all over his face. In fact, he was very close to anger.

"Why would I be telling you about Angie? Who *are* you?"

Kelly stared at him, her first impulse being to take offense at what he'd said. But she stopped herself. This was an agonizing situation. That was why she was trying to fix things. Didn't he see that? But maybe not. Maybe she was intruding and she ought to back off. Still...

She sighed, wishing she knew how to defuse the emotion he was feeling.

"I'm your friend, Joe. I care." Shaking her head, she looked into his eyes. "And I'd like to hear about it." She put a hand on his forearm, trying to calm him. "Just talk about it. I don't have to be there at all. Let her hear you."

The look on his face was stubborn and not at all friendly. "She's too young to understand what the heck I'd be talking about."

"That doesn't matter. And you never know how much children absorb."

He backed away, not accepting her touch. "No, Kelly. It's just not a good idea."

She searched his eyes. Anger was simmering in him just below the surface. She really wasn't sure why this should make him angry. He'd loved Angie. Angie was Mei's mother. What could be more natural than to tell her what her mother was like?

"It's your call, of course, but it just seems to me that talking about her mother, talking with open affection, would help draw her in, help make her feel like this is part of a continuum and not such a strange place, after all."

He shook his head, eyes stormy. "I think you're nuts."

"But Joe…"

"I'm not going to…to talk about…Angie," he said, his voice rough. "I can't."

Kelly's heart twisted and she licked her dry lips. He couldn't? She felt a surge of compassion, but still, that didn't seem right. He was the sort of man who could do anything. Was there more here than she knew? Obviously.

But there was also more at stake. Mei came first.

Still, Kelly couldn't ignore his outrage. What was she doing here? The last thing she wanted to do was torture him more. And yet she couldn't help feeling that he was going at this all wrong. Avoiding pain was often the best way to bring it on at the worst possible time. Her instinct was to try to nudge him out of the self-indulgence of his grief.

Wow, had she really thought that? Pretty tough stuff.

And yet she stood by it. After all, his comfort wasn't what was important anymore. He had a child to think of. He had to do what was best for Mei.

"Okay." Kelly turned back toward the high chair. "As I said, it's your call. If you can't get beyond the pain, there's no point, I guess."

He didn't answer and he didn't meet her gaze. She spent the next few minutes cleaning up Mei's tray and taking her out of the chair, talking softly to her all the time. He stood with his back against the counter, arms folded, looking out through the French doors toward the sliver of ocean visible in the distance. As she walked out, holding Mei's hand while she toddled alongside her, he didn't say a word.

He knew he'd hurt Kelly by his abrupt response, but it couldn't be helped. He felt angry, though not at her. He was pretty damn bitter at life in general. Self-pity wasn't his usual mode, but sometimes the enormity of it all came down on him and he couldn't shake it until it had worked its way through his system. This was one of those times.

Of course, Kelly had no way of knowing that every time he looked at Mei, he saw Angie. And right now, every time he saw Angie in his mind, he saw her dying right in front of him. He knew he had to get over it. He had to wipe the pain and shock and ugliness from his soul so that he could deal with this bright, new, wonderful child.

Kelly thought Mei's obvious rejection of him hurt. And of course, it wasn't fun to be rebuffed by a sweet little child like that. But he didn't blame Mei at all. She sensed his ambivalence, the way he felt torn and twisted inside, the way he almost winced every time he looked at her, and she reacted to it, as any sensitive, intelligent child would. It was going to take time for both of them.

Meanwhile he had Kelly's strange little project of convincing him that he was a prince of a funny little country he couldn't care less about to deal with. The whole thing could have been genuinely annoying if she weren't such a sweetheart. He had to admit, she wasn't exactly hard to look at, either. In fact, he was learning to like her quite a lot.

Moving restlessly, he gave himself a quick lecture on his attitude, ending with a resolution to be nicer to Kelly. Funny thing was, he knew right away it wouldn't be hard at all.

Kelly played with the little girl in her room for the next hour, helping her try out all the toys, and reading to her from a couple of the soft, padded books. Every few minutes, Mei would get up and run around the room, whooping to her own little tune, as though she had untapped energy that needed using up. She was bright, quick and interested in everything. So far she wasn't saying much, but Kelly had a feeling once the floodgates opened, words would come pouring out, even if they weren't understandable to anyone but the child herself.

Kelly spent some time reorganizing the shelves and finding interesting things packed away there, including some pictures and souvenirs that told a story better than Joe had been doing so far.

When Mei fell asleep over her book, Kelly wasn't surprised. She was still very tired from her long trip the day before. Kelly tucked her into bed, picked up a couple of items and went back out.

Joe was taking care of some bills on the Internet, and she waited until he logged off.

"What's up?" he asked, and she was pleased to see his eyes had lost the sheen of vague hostility they'd had when she'd seen him last.

"Mei fell asleep, but she won't be out long. I thought this would be a good time to plan a walk down to the beach."

"Do you think she's ready for that?"

"Sure. I think it would be really exciting for her." She gave him a smile. "Just think of your first time seeing the ocean."

"Kelly, she just came in on a plane over the Pacific," he reminded her.

"But that's not the same as up close and personal."

"No. You're right." He frowned, looking at her. "Will you be able to carry her? You know she still won't let me do it."

"Why would I carry her," she asked with an impish look, "when you've got that huge baby stroller?" She'd seen it standing in the hallway. "It would be a crime to let it go to waste. Like having a Porsche and letting it sit in the driveway."

"Oh." He grinned at the analogy. "That's right. I forgot all about it." His blue eyes softened as he looked at her, his gaze traveling over her face and taking in the whole of her. "Did anybody ever tell you that you brighten a room just by being in it?" he asked softly.

"No," she said, but felt a certain glow at that.

He shook his head, obviously liking what he saw. "I wonder why not."

She liked this man. How could she not? But liking him too much would be fraught with all sorts of dangers, she knew. She had to be very careful to keep things light and impersonal as much as possible.

"Probably because the whole concept is pure fantasy on your part," she said, trying to stick to her intentions with a little good-natured teasing.

But for once, he wasn't really cooperating. Instead of joining in the mockery, his look became more intense.

"No, it's not." Reaching out, he touched her curly hair, and his smile was wistful for a moment. "Tell me why you came looking for me, Kelly. Why you spent so much time watching me. I still don't understand it."

She looked up into his eyes. How could she explain? Did he really want to hear about her work at the Ambrian News Agency, about how her parents had raised her with a love of Ambria, how she'd studied the royal family for over a year before she saw his picture and knew instantly that he looked remarkably like one of the missing Ambrian princes would at this age? About how she'd fought everyone in her agency for this assignment, and then finally decided to come out on her own time, on her own money, to see for herself if what her intuition had told her was really true?

She might as well cut right to the chase.

"I work for an agency that gathers intelligence."

"What kind of intelligence?"

"Information. Things of interest to the exiled Ambrian community."

He frowned. "Why are they exiled?"

"Because of the people who took over Ambria twenty-five years ago. The coup was pretty bloody, but a lot of people escaped. There's a rather large group of us living in this country. More are scattered all over Europe."

He nodded, seeming to think that over. "So these folks who took over—are they some sort of oppressive regime?"

"Absolutely."

"Hmm. So what do you do at this agency? Don't tell me you're a secret agent—an undercover operative, perhaps?"

She glared at him. "What if I am?"

He grinned. "Well, there's really nothing I can say that wouldn't get me into trouble on that one. So I'll just keep my thoughts to myself."

"Don't worry. I'm not an agent. I'm an analyst."

"That's a relief." He paused. "So what does an analyst do?"

"I pretty much sit in a room and read articles in newspapers and magazines, and try to figure out what is actually going on in Ambria. I analyze information and write reports for policy makers."

"Sounds like a great job. But what does this have to do with me?"

She gave him a wise look. "Over time, I've developed a theory about you."

"You're not the first."

She hid her smile. "I'm sure I'm not."

He looked at her quizzically. "How about a short wrap-up on this theory thing? I've got to get going on some more paperwork, and I don't have time for anything long and involved."

She shook her head. "Never mind. You'll just laugh. Again."

"Laugh at you? Never."

Enough people had already laughed about her theory. For some reason, Kelly couldn't stand mockery from him right now. She had to be on firmer ground with her ideas of his being Ambrian royalty before she told him the whole story. He'd already told her she was crazy to think he might be an Ambrian prince. She wasn't going to go into that again right now. But she could try to get him to understand why she wanted so much to unravel this mystery.

"Do you ever do crossword puzzles?" she asked him.

He nodded. "There was a period of time during my recuperation when I felt like I was a prisoner in that hospital bed. But I had my crossword puzzles, and that was all I did, night and day."

She smiled. "So you know what it's like when you're almost finished with a puzzle, all except for one block of words. You look the hints up, you try different things, nothing works right. You try to put it aside and forget it, but you can't. No matter what you do or where you go that day, you keep fooling with that puzzle, trying different answers out in your mind. And then, suddenly, a piece of the tangle becomes clear and you think you have the key to the whole thing." She looked at him expectantly. "Has that ever happened to you?"

"Sure. All the time."

"You're so certain you have the correct answer," she went on, driving home her point, "but you can't prove it until you go back and find the puzzle and write in the words and see for yourself. Right?"

"Sure."

She threw out her hands. "That's what I'm doing here. I'm trying to prove I found the right answer to the puzzle."

He nodded, frowning thoughtfully at the same time. "So tell me, am I the answer or the puzzle?"

She grinned at him. "Both right now."

Their gazes met and held, and she felt her pulse begin to race in her veins. There was something between them. She could feel it. All her stern warnings to herself about not getting involved melted away. She wanted to kiss him. That desire grew in her quickly and was stronger than she'd ever felt it. Every part of her wanted to reach out to him, to come closer, to hold on and feel the heat. Attraction was evolving into compulsion. Her brain was closing off and her senses were sharpening. His warm, beautiful mouth was becoming her only focus.

Joe looked down at her eyes, her skin, her lips, and he was suddenly overwhelmed with the urge to kiss her. Would she stop him? It wouldn't be that unusual if he were to try to lose this lingering unhappiness in a woman's love.

Well, "love" would be asking a bit much at this stage.

How about losing it in a woman's warm, soft body? Not unusual—it happened all the time. What if he took her in his arms and held her close and let his male instincts come back to life...?

He looked into her eyes again and saw the questions there, but also saw the hint of acceptance. Reaching out, he slipped his hand behind her head, his fingers in her hair, and began to pull her toward him. Her eyes widened, but she didn't resist. His gaze settled on her mouth, and he felt a quick, strong pulse of desire, taking his breath away.

For the moment, she was his for the asking. But what gave him the right to be asking? This wasn't the way it should be. She deserved better. She deserved real love, and that was something he couldn't give her.

What the hell was he doing? Had he lost all sense of decency and self-control? He pulled his hand back and, instead of kissing her, turned away without a word. He felt nothing but self-loathing.

Kelly stood very still, watching him go, feeling such a deep, empty sense of loss that she ached with it. He'd been about to kiss her. What had stopped him? She knew very well what ought to keep *her* from kissing *him*. But what was his excuse?

Taking a deep, cleansing breath, she turned back toward Mei's room and tried to calm her emotions, settle her jumping nerves. If kissing was out, she might as well start preparing for their walk.

CHAPTER SIX

THE SUN SHONE on everything. There wasn't a hint of fog. The sky was blue and the ocean was even bluer. It was a beautiful day.

"I see why they call it the Golden State," Kelly noted. "Everything seems to shimmer with gold on a day like this."

Joe nodded, gazing out to sea and pulling fresh sea air deep into his lungs. He loved the beach. Turning, he glanced at Kelly. She looked good here, as if she belonged.

"I called Angie's family in the Philippines," he told her. "They say they have no idea what happened to the nanny. I got the impression that they couldn't care less."

"You'd think they would want to know Mei was okay."

He sighed. "It's a long story, Kelly. Angie's family didn't ever like me much, and they act like they've written Mei off now that she's with me." He shrugged. "But that's a problem for another time."

Kelly couldn't imagine how anyone could see Mei

and want to forget her. But she quickly pushed that aside. Mei took up all her attention at the moment.

As they strolled down the promenade, Mei sat like a little princess, watching everything with huge eyes. She didn't cringe when Joe came near anymore, but she definitely wanted Kelly to be in her range of vision at all times, and would call out if she lost sight of her. She loved the ocean. When they took her close enough to see the waves, she bounced up and down with excitement and clapped her hands.

Mei was a treat to watch, and Kelly glanced at Joe every so often to make sure he was enjoying it, too. He gave every indication of growing pride in his adorable child.

"Look at how smart she is," he kept saying. "See how she knows what that is? See how she called the dog over? See how she stops and thinks before she calls you?"

She did all those things. The trouble was, she didn't call *him*. And Kelly knew that was breaking his heart.

They bought tacos at a food stand for lunch, then stopped by a viewing platform to sit down and eat them. Kelly had brought along some baby food in a jar for Mei. The child took the food willingly enough, but then would forget to swallow. There was just too much to look at. She didn't have time for the distractions.

They finished eating, and when they weren't staring at the wild and beautiful surf, they sat back and watched Mei watch the people strolling by.

"I've never been to Ambria," Kelly told Joe. "But

from the pictures I've seen, the beaches look a lot like this."

He turned to glance at her, then sighed and leaned back as though getting ready for a long ordeal.

"Okay, Kelly," he said, as if giving in on something he'd been fighting. "Lay it on me. Tell me all about Ambria. I'm going to need the basics. I really don't know a thing."

She gazed at him, suddenly hit by the awesome responsibility he'd given her. If he really was the prince and she was going to be the person who introduced him to his country, she'd better get this right.

Clearing her throat, she searched her memory wildly, trying to think of the best way to approach this.

"Nothing fancy," he warned. "And don't take forever. Just the facts, ma'am."

She took a deep breath and decided to start at the beginning. "Okay. Here goes." She put on a serious face. "You know where Ambria is located. And you know it's a relatively isolated island nation. The DeAngelis family ruled the country for hundreds of years, starting in the days of the Holy Roman Empire, when the Crusades were just beginning. Their monarchy was one of the longest standing ever. Until twenty-five years ago, when it ended."

"And why did it end?" he asked, sounding interested despite himself.

"The vicious Granvilli clan had been their rivals for years and years. Most of their plots had failed, but finally, they got lucky. They invaded under the guise of popular liberation, gained a foothold and burned the castle. The royal family had to flee for their lives."

"Yikes," he murmured, frowning.

"Yikes, indeed," she responded, leaning forward. "They sent their children into hiding with other families sworn to secrecy. The king and queen…" She paused, realizing she might be talking about his parents. "They were killed, but only after having arranged for it to be widely believed that all their children had been killed, as well."

"So as to keep them safe from the Granvillis," he said softly, absorbing it all.

"Yes. If the Granvillis knew they were still alive, they would have tried to find them and kill them, to wipe out any natural opposition to their rule. That's why the children are called the lost princes."

"How many are there?"

"There were five sons and two daughters, but no one knows how many might have survived."

"If any did," he reminded her.

"Of course. Remnants of the old ruling order do exist, but none of them know for sure what happened to the royal children. There are refugee communities of Ambrians in many parts of Europe and the U.S.A. Reunions are held periodically in the old Roman town of Piasa, high in the northern mountains, where they say the oldsters talk and drink and dream about what might have been." She paused for a moment, her eyes dreamy as she pictured the scene. "Meanwhile, most of the younger generation have gone on with their lives and are modern, integrated Europeans and Americans,

many quite successful in international trade and com-
merce."

He nodded, taking it all in with a faraway look in his
eyes, just as she had—almost as though he was sharing
her vision.

"So what about these lost princes?" he ventured.
"What's happened to them?"

"Lately, rumors have surfaced that some of them did
survive. These rumors have become all the rage. They've
really ignited the memories of the oldsters and put a
spark in the speculative ideas of the younger generation.
Ambria has been a dark place, shrouded in mystery and
set apart from modern life, for twenty-five years. It's a
tragedy for history and for our people. Ambrians burn
to get their nation back."

He laughed shortly. "Sure, the older ones want a
return to the old ways, no doubt, and the younger ones
want the romance of a revolution. Human nature."

She frowned. She didn't much like his reducing it to
something so ordinary.

"Every Ambrian I know is passionately devoted to
getting rid of the usurper regime," she said stoutly.

He grunted. "Mainly the oldsters, I'll bet."

"Sure. Don't they count?"

He shrugged. "Go on."

"Different factions have been vying for power and
followers, each with their own ideas of how an invasion
might be launched. The conviction has grown that this
can only happen if we can find one of the lost royals
still alive. Believe me, the ex-pat community is buzzing
with speculation."

"Like honeybees," he murmured.

That put her back up a little. "You can make fun of it if you want to, but people are ready to move. The Granvillis have ruled the country badly. They're really considered terrible despots. They've got to go."

Her voice rose a bit as she tried to convince him, and he turned and grinned. "A regular Joan of Arc, aren't you?" he commented.

She colored. "No, of course not. But I don't think you understand how passionate a lot of exiled Ambrians are about this."

He sat up straighter and looked cynical. "Yeah, sure. People are totally passionate in the talking and threatening phase. It's when you put a gun in their hand and say, 'Okay, go do it,' that they suddenly remember something they have to take care of at home."

She swallowed back her first response. After all, he'd actually been one of the ones doing the fighting. He knew a whole heck of a lot more about that than she did.

"Maybe so," she said. "But something has happened that is threatening to put a lot of Ambrians in one place at one time, and if one of the princes shows up..." She shrugged.

He looked up at that, curious in spite of himself. "What are you talking about?"

"Here's what's going on." She leaned forward almost conspiratorially. "The old duke, Nathanilius, has died. He was the brother of the king who was killed during the invasion, and was considered the titular head of the family. The funeral is being planned in Piasa, and it threatens to be chaotic—no one knows who will show up, but they expect a lot of people who haven't been seen in years." Kelly gazed at Joe significantly. "The question is, who will try to seize the mantle of the old regime? Will the Granvillis try to disrupt the ceremony or even assassinate any of the DeAngelis loyaltists who will come out of hiding for the event? It's a pretty exciting time." She smiled. "Dangerous, too."

Some of his cynicism melted away. "Wow. Interesting."

"Yes."

He frowned, thinking. "Twenty-five years ago."

"You would have been about four, right?"

He merely nodded, looking out at the ocean. Memories—yeah, he had a few. He wasn't about to tell her, but he did have some pictures in his head from when he was very young. He remembered a fire. He remembered fear. He remembered being in a boat in the dark. The sound of oars splashing in inky water.

But were they really his own memories? That was the trouble with these things. How much was from tales he'd been told and how much from stories he'd made up himself when he was a boy? He had a feeling he knew what she would say about them. But he wasn't ready to surrender to her royal dreams.

He wasn't sure he wanted to be a prince.

Besides, he had other things on his mind, the most important of which was finding a way to get his daughter to like him. He was getting better at looking at her without feeling Angie's tragic presence. That should help.

He had no doubt she'd sensed that from the beginning, and that had helped fuel her reaction to him.

In some ways he was torn. Anything that reminded him of Angie should be good, shouldn't it? And yet it didn't quite work out that way. He'd loved her so much. Losing her had been hard. But that was hardly Mei's problem.

When you came right down to it, he himself was probably the roadblock to happiness there. He was pretty sure Kelly thought so. The baby was getting vibes from him, a sense of his pain, and she didn't like it. Who could blame her? The thing was, how to get it to stop before it became a habit she wouldn't ever shake? She couldn't distrust him forever.

They walked slowly home, enjoying the adorable things Mei did. People stopped them to say how cute she was. Dogs came up wagging their tails. Even the seagulls that swooped overhead seemed to be screaming her name. When one came especially close, then wheeled and almost lost its balance, Joe and Kelly looked at each other and laughed.

This was real life. This was pretty good.

But Joe's smile faded as he thought of Angie and how she'd never had a chance to live this way with her baby. On impulse, he reached for Mei's hand, hoping she would curl it around his finger. For just a second, she seemed about to try.

But then she realized it was his, and she pulled back and began to cry. Huge, rolling tears sprang instantly into her eyes. Kelly bent over to quiet her, but nothing was going to work this time.

"She's tired." Kelly looked up at Joe apologetically as she lifted Mei out of the stroller. "Don't take it to heart."

"Don't take it to heart?" Had she really said that? A dark sense of despair filled him and he turned away. How could he not take it to heart?

"Joe, I need to give her a bath. Then I'll read her a book and let her play before I put her down for a nap. Maybe you could come in and watch her play? Or maybe even read to her?"

"Yeah, sure," he said. "Maybe."

Kelly watched Joe walk away, and knew he had no intention of doing either of those things. Her heart ached for him, but she went ahead with her plans. Mei loved her bath and liked pointing out the animals in her books while Kelly read to her. She was ready for sleep by the time Kelly put her down. And just as she'd foreseen, Joe never showed up.

She searched until she found him in the garage, waxing down his surfboard.

"You didn't come in to see Mei playing," she said, trying not to make it come out like an accusation, but failing utterly.

He glanced up at her with haunted eyes and looked completely guilty. "I know. What's she doing right now?"

"She's asleep."

He threw down his cloth. "Okay. I'll go in and watch her for awhile a bit later."

Kelly frowned, not convinced he really meant it. This did not bode well. But she had no hold over him. She couldn't make him do something he didn't want to do, could she?

"I'm going to take this opportunity, while she's asleep, to run over to my motel and get a few things. Okay?"

"Sure." He took another swipe at his board. "Do you need my car?"

"No. It's only a couple of blocks away. And anyway, I've got my rental car there. I guess I might as well drive back in it."

Kelly hesitated for a moment, then pulled one of the items she'd found in the room out of a shopping bag she'd brought along. It was the framed photograph of a lovely young woman.

"Is this Angie?" she asked bluntly, holding up the picture.

His head snapped back and his eyes narrowed. "Where did you find that?" he demanded gruffly.

"In Mei's room, packed away on a shelf."

He stared at it, nodding slowly. "Yes. That's Angie."

"I thought so. When I showed it to Mei, she said, 'Mama.' And she smiled. So she obviously knew who it was."

Joe grunted. He didn't have to ask what her point was. He knew.

"She's lovely," Kelly said, looking at the photo. "She looks like a wonderful person."

He nodded. "She was," he said softly.

Kelly looked into his face with real determination. "She deserves to be talked about and treated like a real woman, not an icon on a pedestal. Can't you see that, Joe?"

He nodded again, clearly a little surprised by her vehemence. "Of course."

She drew in a deep breath, then stepped closer.

"You know, Joe, I've had bad things happen. I've had periods of unhappiness when I wondered 'Why me?' I've spent some time drowning in depression."

She looked up to see if he was listening. He seemed to be.

"But I began to read about a psychologist who has a theory that we very much make our own happiness and our own unhappiness. One thing he suggests doing is to act like you're happy, even when you're not. Go through the motions. Pretend. It can seem awkward at first, but the more you do it, the more it begins to come true. Reality follows the form. In a way, you're teaching yourself happiness. And if you work hard enough at it, it can become a part of you, a part of your being."

He was looking skeptical, but he was listening.

"I'm sure it doesn't always work, but it worked pretty well for me."

He peered into her eyes for a moment, then went back to rubbing the surface of his board. "That sounds like a lot of new age garbage."

"Fine. Call it names if it makes you feel better. But it made a real difference in my life." Kelly started toward the door and said flippantly, over her shoulder, "Just sayin'."

Joe kept pretending to work until he heard her go out the front door, then he slumped against the wall and closed his eyes. Why the hell had he let this woman into his life to challenge all his attitudes and assumptions? He'd been thinking about almost nothing else since she'd made her crazy suggestion that morning in the kitchen that he talk about Angie.

He'd been angry with Kelly at first, but deep down, he knew it was inevitable that he do it at some point. After all, he had Angie's baby here. Someday she would want to know all about her mother. Was he going to be able to tell her everything?

Kelly wanted him to get started right away, but she didn't know about what had happened in that jungle. How did you explain to a little girl about how her mother had died and why? Would Mei learn to blame him?

He blamed himself, so why not?

But of course Kelly was right. What was he thinking? It wasn't all about death. It wasn't all about pain and unhappy endings. He'd had many full, rich, happy experiences with Angie that had had nothing to do with the painful part. There'd been love and affection and music and flowers and boat rides on the lake and swimming to the waterfall. It was way past time he let himself dwell on that part of the past, not the horror at the end.

He finished up his work on the surfboard whistling a tune he didn't recognize at first. He knew it was an old song, but where had it come from? And then the words spilled out in his head. "Pretend you're happy when you're blue," it began. Then something about it not being hard to do. He groaned. Even his own brain was against him.

* * *

Kelly wasn't gone long, though she stopped at the market for some baby supplies. But when she got back, something felt wrong. She stopped and listened. Nothing. At least Mei wasn't awake and crying.

She started toward the bedroom, but something stopped her. There was a rustling. There, she heard it again. The sound was coming from a room she assumed was a den, and something about it seemed downright furtive.

Setting down the bags she'd brought, Kelly walked toward the room as quietly as she could and gave the unlatched door a little push. It opened without a creak, and she saw a tall, curvaceous, platinum-blonde woman with a superstar tan going through a large wooden file cabinet. She had her cell phone to her ear at the same time and was talking softly.

"I'm telling you, there's not even a picture book about Ambria around here. Nothing. I can't find one little hint that he even knows what the country is."

Suddenly the woman realized someone was in the doorway, and she whirled to face Kelly, staring into her astonished eyes.

"Uh, talk to you later," she said into the phone. "I've gotta go." She snapped it shut.

"What are you doing?" Kelly demanded.

"Well, hello." The woman said with a smile. She was quite attractive in a tight-bodiced, bleached-blonde, fire-engine-red lipstick sort of way. But somehow, Kelly missed the appeal.

"Why are you going through Joe's things?" she demanded. She was pretty sure she already knew who this was, but it would be nice to have confirmation.

"Oh!" The woman looked stunned that she might be suspected of doing anything wrong. Her eyes widened in faux innocence. "I'm not. Not really. I just wanted to see how Joe had his files set up, because I'm going to be giving him a bid on renovating this den, doing a little decorating, and I wanted to see—" she waved a hand majestically "—I wanted to see how he works."

Kelly didn't buy it for a minute. Frowning, she balanced on the balls of her feet, feeling fierce and protective. "You were going through his files."

The woman was beginning to lose some of that overweening self-confidence she exuded. She actually looked a little worried.

"No. Oh no. I was checking things over so that…"

"Hey, Kelly. You made it back."

It was probably a good thing that Joe appeared at this point. Kelly was not in a forgiving mood. He came into the room carrying a large screwdriver and looking from one woman to the other.

"I was just putting up a growth chart for Mei in the bathroom," he explained, then frowned. "What's the problem?"

Kelly pointed accusingly in the woman's direction. "She was going through your files."

Joe appeared bemused. "Was she? But Kelly, I basically told her to." He gave her an indulgent smile, as though she were a little kid who just didn't get it. "This is Sonja. The woman who did such a great job on Mei's room. She's just looking around, trying to get the lay of the land in case I hire her to redecorate my living areas."

Oh no, she wasn't. Joe hadn't seen what Kelly had seen, heard what she'd heard. She had caught Sonja going through the files, and now she wanted to know exactly what she'd been looking for.

"This was a lot more than merely surveying the work space," she began.

He didn't want to hear it. "Listen, I'm sure it's a mis-understanding. She's okay. I knew she was going to be snooping around, getting ideas."

Sonja sensed victory and she smiled like the Cheshire cat. Kelly bit her lip in frustration. She couldn't under-stand why Joe didn't see that.

"Sonja, this is Kelly," he was saying, as though intro-ducing two women he was sure would be fast friends. "She's helping me out with Mei, since the nanny didn't show up."

"I'm so glad you got someone." The tall, beautiful woman tossed her hair back and turned her dazzling smile on Joe. "I'd volunteer myself, but you know how it is. I'm good at kiddy decorating but I don't know a thing about actually taking care of the little darlings." She glanced Kelly's way. "I leave that to nannies like your friend here."

"I'm not a nanny," Kelly stated.

"Well, you're doing nanny work, aren't you?" she noted, never taking her eyes off Joe.

"What's wrong with child care?" Kelly asked, at a loss as to why the woman would be saying that with just a hint of disdain. "Every mother on earth does it."

Sonja had obviously grown bored with the conversation. She rolled her eyes in Joe's direction, then sighed. "Well, I'm going to have to get going. Places to go, promises to keep. You know how it is." Her slick smile was all for Joe. "But don't forget, we need to get together and go over my ideas. And talk about my tour plans—plans I'm hoping to rope you into." She gave him a flirtatious smile. "In the meantime, don't forget you owe me a dinner." She tapped her index finger on his chest. "You promised."

Joe was grinning back, basking in all this obvious admiration. It made Kelly's blood boil to see how easily he seemed to fall for it.

"Sure," he said happily. "We'll have to see what we can do to keep that promise."

"I'm looking forward to it."

To Kelly's shock, the woman leaned close and gave Joe a kiss on the cheek, then turned and winked insolently in Kelly's direction. Her attitude very plainly said, *Don't think you've got this one on the line yet, sister. I've got skills you can only dream of.*

She started out, and Joe gave Kelly a happy shrug, then turned back to his carpentry job in the bathroom. Kelly hesitated a moment, then decided to go after Sonja. That woman had some explaining to do.

CHAPTER SEVEN

"WAIT A MINUTE," Kelly said from the curb as Sonja reached for her car door.

The woman turned back with a frown, and Kelly hesitated again. She wanted to accuse her, wanted to question her, but didn't want to do anything that would make Sonja think she was right to suspect Joe had a connection to Ambria. Kelly had to be very careful here.

"No matter what Joe thinks, you and I both know you were searching for information in his files."

She shrugged, putting on her huge dark sunglasses. "Like he said, you misunderstood."

"No. I heard you on the phone, talking about some sort of evidence of a connection you were looking for. If you want to know something about Joe, why can't you just ask him to his face?"

"My dear, once again, you've misunderstood."

"Have I?"

"Yes. Don't you worry your little head about all this. Just take good care of that baby." And she slipped into the car and drove off.

Kelly drew a deep breath. This wasn't good. She was sure of what she'd heard when she'd entered into that room. If Sonja wasn't after Joe because she thought he was Ambrian, she was after him for something else. At any rate, he had to be prepared for whatever was going to be coming down the pike.

Kelly went back into the house and slipped into Mei's room to check on her. The precious child was sound asleep, and Kelly watched her for a moment, wondering what her life would be like. Surely she would warm to Joe soon. He would hire a good nanny and their life together would develop over time. Something inside Kelly yearned to know the outcome, but she knew she probably never would. That was all in the future, however. She was more concerned with keeping them both—Joe and Mei—safe right now. And that was really beginning to worry her.

She had to convince Joe that his friend Sonja was not on the up and up. Slipping back out of Mei's room, Kelly searched for Joe and finally found him just finishing up.

Not giving him time to distract her with jokes, she quickly told him about what she'd heard Sonja say on the phone, and when she'd confronted her a few minutes later. He listened, nodding and looking interested, but he didn't act like a man ready to jump in the car and head for higher ground.

"She was sent here for a reason. I'm sure of it, Joe. She suspects something. She was hunting for evidence of an Ambrian connection."

He was picking up his tools and looking rather proud of the new wooden measuring chart he'd affixed to the wall. Instead of being concerned about what she was saying, he stood back and admired it.

"Well, since I don't have any evidence of an Ambrian connection," he said casually, making a tiny adjustment to the way the chart was hanging, "she's out of luck, isn't she?"

"But don't you see? Just the fact that there are suspicions shows the danger you're in."

He raised one dark eyebrow as he gazed at her cynically. "As a matter of fact, Kelly, the only evidence of an Ambrian connection around here is you."

She opened her mouth but no words came out. What could she say to that? In a way, he was right.

"I hope you were discreet," he added with a hint of laughter in his blue eyes.

"Yes, Joe. I was very discreet." She shook her head as she thought of the last person who had warned her of that. "So discreet, Jim would have been proud of me."

He frowned. "Who's Jim?"

She sighed. "My boss. The one who told me not to come looking for you."

His flash of a grin was electric. "I'm glad you're such a disobedient worker."

She looked up in surprise and her gaze met his and held. That electricity was still there and it sparked between them for just a second, making her nerves tingle and her heart beat a little faster.

She turned away. She didn't want to feel this sort of spicy provocation. This wasn't why she was here.

But she needed to make some things clear to him, and she wasn't sure how she was going to do it. She had to explain more firmly to Joe what this was all about—that he might just have that elusive Ambrian connection, and if he did, he had to face the consequences of that fact. Because those consequences could be lethal.

Turning back, she steeled herself and looked at him sternly. "Joe, you need to listen to me, and you need to take what I say seriously. No kidding around."

The humor drained from his eyes and he waited, poised. She blinked at him in wonder. He was actually receptive to what she had to say. She felt a rush of affection for him and that only made it all so much harder.

Kelly sucked in a deep breath. "I think you have to get out of here. I think you have to go."

His face hardened. "What are you talking about?"

"They've found you," she said earnestly, trying to convince him. "These people—Sonja and whoever she was talking to on the phone—must be either representatives of the Granvilli clan or someone in sympathy with them. Joe, you can't stay here. You can't risk it."

He was frowning. "Risk what? Kelly, I'm not your prince. I'm not *their* prince, either."

"But you see…" She stopped, tortured and not sure how she was going to convince him. "It doesn't even matter if you are or you aren't. If the Granvillis think you're one of the princes, it's the same as if you are. And they'll probably try to kill you."

There. The words were out. She gazed at him, hardly believing she'd actually said it. He stared back, his eyes cold as ice. She couldn't tell what he was thinking, but he took his time giving her an answer, so she knew he had to be considering what she'd said.

"Listen, Kelly," he replied at last, "I've got a few skills in the hopper. I think I can take care of any threat of that kind." He smiled, but there was no humor in it. "I'm not exactly a sitting duck."

She shook her head. She had no doubt he could hold his own in a fair fight. She knew he was a trained warrior. But that didn't mean he could guard against everything. Why did he refuse to understand?

"You can't fight off the secret service of a whole country on your own," she told him ardently.

He looked pained. "Now you're being melodramatic. Slow down. Take it easy. I'm not going anywhere."

"You can't just think of yourself now, you know," she added, trying to drive her fears home to him. "You have Mei to consider."

"Of course." A slight frown wrinkled the skin between his brows. "I'm very aware of that."

"Are you?" She felt tears prickling her eyelids. Why wasn't she better at expressing just how serious this was?

Joe took her by the shoulders and looked down into her face. "You want me to run off and hide somewhere because a woman I hired to decorate my baby's room looks at me and thinks of Ambria." He shook his head as though he just couldn't buy it. "How do you know she isn't one of the good guys? Why are you so sure she didn't emigrate as a refugee, just like your parents and you? How do you know she doesn't want to recruit me into fighting the Granvillis just like you do?"

He had her there. Kelly had no idea, no evidence at all. But she had a very strong feeling. Still, held here in his grip, she could only look up at his beautiful face and wonder why he wouldn't let her save him.

"I'm not getting into anyone else's wars," he told her, searching her eyes as though he thought he might find something to reassure him there. "I've had enough of that. Enough for a lifetime."

"Joe, I...I understand...I..." She was babbling. What else could she do? He was so close Kelly could feel the heat from his body. Her head was full of his clean, masculine scent and her heart was beating like a drum. She couldn't think straight, couldn't manage a coherent sentence. All she could do was stare at the beautiful smooth and tanned skin revealed by the opening in his shirt. Her head felt light and she was afraid she was going to pass out.

Suddenly, as though he'd realized he was holding her shoulders and wasn't sure why, he pulled his hands away and she swayed before him, blinking rapidly and trying to catch her breath.

"Are you okay?" he asked.

She nodded, embarrassed beyond belief. "Yes," she managed to say. "I'm okay. Really."

"I'm sorry to be so adamant about this, Kelly," he told her, his brow still furrowed. "I've got my own problems, and I'm not in the mood for more."

"Of course not," she murmured, but he was already turning away. She watched him go, and slowly began to regain equilibrium, glad he had been too wrapped up in their argument to notice what a fool she was making of herself. She'd never realized she could be such an easy mark for a sexy man. She was going to have to be more careful.

Inhaling another deep breath, she got back with the program. Something had to be done to convince Joe to take the threat of harm more seriously. Kelly thought for a moment, then nodded and went straight for her cell phone. Time to call in the cavalry on this one.

When her boss answered, she smiled, glad to hear his voice again.

"So, Kelly, how's it going, anyway? Found any more princes out there in sunny California?" He chuckled.

She had to bite her lip to keep from reacting sharply. She was so tired of being the focus of all their joking at the agency. "Princes, princesses, earls, dukes. They're a dime a dozen out here, Jim. You ought to come out and find one for yourself."

"Hey, I thought you were going to San Diego. Not Hollywood."

"Cute." She sighed. "Actually, I think Joe is the real deal. I just haven't been able to convince him of it yet."

There was a pause, then Jim said, "You mean he doesn't know if he is or isn't?"

"Nope."

"Wow. That's a new one."

"Yes, it is. And pretty frustrating."

"Hmm." Jim seemed to agree. "But tell me this. If he doesn't know the truth, who does?"

"I do. And apparently someone else suspects as well. Jim, can you do a little research for me? I need some background on a woman calling herself Sonja Smith."

She heard him choke on his cup of coffee, and sighed. "Yes, I know. It's not likely to be her real name. But she's affiliated with a baby boutique here in San Diego." She gave him the rest of what she knew, and he agreed, reluctantly, to look into it for her.

"Don't expect too much," he said in his droll way. "In my experience, every Madame Smith tends to evaporate as soon as you shine a light on her."

"I know. But she's been prodding Joe about Ambria. Now how many people without ulterior motives are likely to be doing that?"

"Not many," he agreed. "Of course, there's you."

She groaned. "Spare me the lecture. I've already heard it."

He snickered and Kelly felt her face go hot. How she would love to prove all the naysayers she worked with wrong!

"Okay, now here's a question for you," Jim said. "When are you coming back?"

"Back?" Her hand tightened on her phone. "I'll be in on Monday. Why?"

"Because it turns out half the office will be going to the funeral in Piasa. We're going to need you here to cover."

Kelly frowned. "What's going on?"

"It looks like one of your lost princes really has shown up."

"What?" Her heart leaped.

"There are rumors that Prince Darius has been seen."

"No!"

"Seems he was living with a family in Holland for many years, then he was a businessman in London."

This was fantastic news. All these months, ever since she'd presented the people she worked for with an outline of her theory on what might have happened to the lost princes, she'd had nothing but doubt and ridicule thrown her way. If they began to show up, her vindication would be sweet.

"And all the time, no one knew."

"That seems to be the case." Jim cleared his throat. "And now he's on his way to Piasa, as is just about everyone in the Ambrian universe."

"Except me." She knew she had no hope of getting the assignment. She was the lowest level employee there, and would be left behind to cover for everyone else. That went without saying. But she could dream, couldn't she?

"I'm not going, either. We'll be here analyzing the dispatches. You know the drill."

"Indeed."

"So, when can you get back?"

"Saturday is the very soonest I can manage."

"Make it early on Saturday. This isn't a joke, Kelly. We're really going to need you."

This news was so exciting, Kelly wanted to dance all the way back to Mei's room. She wanted to tell Joe, but she stopped herself. Not yet. First, she had to show him that there was really a reason he should care.

Mei was still asleep, so Kelly went out to the entryway to pick up some of the packages she'd brought. First she changed out of the clothes she'd worn for two days now, and put on a pair of snug jeans and a cropped seersucker top that showed off a bit of belly button. She spent a few minutes putting baby food into a cupboard, then went out on the deck, where Joe was reading a newspaper.

"What have you heard about the nanny?" Kelly asked him.

He turned and smiled in a way that let her know he liked how she looked out here in the late afternoon sun.

"She'll be here tomorrow afternoon."

"Oh. Good. I hope I'll have time to train her on what Mei likes."

He gave her a lopsided grin. "You've already become an expert on that, have you?"

She answered with a jaunty tilt of her chin. "Sort of."

The truth was, she was falling in love with the child. But since doing so was crazy and would only lead to more heartbreak, she kept quiet about it. Why tell him, anyway?

"Mrs. Gomez is her name. A good friend of mine runs this agency. She'll make sure she's completely vetted. I trust her judgment."

Kelly nodded, biting her lower lip. If she was really honest, she would admit that she didn't relish the prospect of someone else taking over Mei's care.

"The first thing to notice is if she starts asking any questions about Ambria," she pointed out as she made her way to the railing and leaned against it, looking toward the ocean.

"You got it. We don't trust those Ambria-asking people."

She turned her head to glare at him. "This is serious, Joe. Your friend Sonja might just use her influence to stick a ringer in, someone who would spy for the regime. You never know."

"Ah, come on," he said, rising to join her at the railing. The sun was low in the sky and a beautiful sunset was promising to develop. "Even Sonja has her good points."

From the thread of amusement in his voice, Kelly knew he was goading her just for the fun of it. She could either challenge him or play along. She gave him a sideways look and impulsively decided on the latter.

"Wow, you were bowled over by her beauty, weren't you?" she said accusingly.

He shrugged, his eyelids heavy as he looked at her. "You've got to admit she's pretty nice to look at."

"Right." Kelly made a face. "No wonder the Mata Hari types succeed so well with the dopey gender. Men are totally blinded by beauty. To the point where they ignore danger."

He managed to look innocent as the driven snow. "Well, yes. What's wrong with that?"

If only he was as innocent as he looked. She forced back a smile. "Men are just clueless. Babes in the woods. Easy prey for the machinations of the fairer sex."

"Is that how you see me?"

She threw out her hands. "If the shoe fits…"

His eyes narrowed cynically. "Well, Kelly, my dear,

look who's talking. I mean, you've clearly got a crush on me."

Her mouth dropped at that outrageous statement. "I do not!"

"Really? Why not?"

His expression was endearingly surprised and woebegone, and she had to laugh, knowing he was teasing her.

"You're crazy," she told him. "I'm just trying to warn you to beware of Sonja."

"Sure. That comes through loud and clear." He moved a little closer so that their shoulders were touching. "Are you sure you're not jealous?" he asked softly, as though it was a secret he was sharing with her.

"Jealous?" she practically squealed. "Why would I be jealous?"

He looked at her for a long moment, smiling, then shrugged. "You got me there."

She cleared her throat, a bit relieved. "Exactly."

They stayed there for a few minutes, side by side, neither speaking. The sun touched to the ocean, turning the water red and painting the sky in peaches and crimson. Kelly had a wild fantasy of turning to look into Joe's eyes and curling into his arms. The thought almost stopped her heart cold. She bit her lip and wished it away.

Whether he believed it or not, he was a prince of the Ambrian realm. He wasn't for the taking. She had to keep her thoughts away from such things.

Finding out the truth about his heritage and making sure he knew how to make the most of it—that was what she was really here for. The fact that he was about the handsomest man she'd ever seen beyond the silver screen had nothing to do with it. Nothing at all.

She sighed and turned to go in and check on Mei, but he stopped her with a hand on her upper arm.

"Kelly, tell me why," he said, and as she looked into his eyes, it seemed to her they were haunted by some lingering emotion she couldn't quite identify.

"Why what?" she asked, though she knew.

He swept his arm in a wide arch. "Why all this? Why you're here. Why you want to do this." He shook his head, his gaze searching hers. "But most of all, why you're so intent on putting me up as royalty on a tiny little godforsaken island no one goes to."

She licked her dry lips and searched for the words to explain, words that would convince him what he had to do.

"I told you I'm an analyst for the Ambrian News Agency. I'm the newest, youngest employee, even though I've been there almost two years now. Everybody treats me like a kid."

He pulled back his hand and she returned to leaning on the rail next to him.

"Everything interesting goes to one of the men. Every time a juicy assignment comes up, it's the usual, 'Sorry, dear, we need someone with experience for this one.' And when I ask how I'm supposed to get experience if no one lets me try, all I get are blank stares."

He nodded. "The old Catch 22."

"Exactly. So I decided to pick something no one else was working on, and make it my special field of expertise." She turned to look directly into his eyes. "I picked you."

He laughed and shook his head.

"I'd already been reading a lot about Ambria, and when I picked up a book about the possibility that there were lost children from the old regime who might still be alive, I knew right away this was it. I started finding out everything I could about them. About you."

He looked skeptical. "Did you find any evidence that they really exist?"

She hesitated. "Well, nothing solid. Not then. But I've read everything I could find on the speculation and the rumors. And I've interviewed a few people who think it's possible. And..."

She stopped. She wasn't ready to tell him about his brother Darius being sighted yet.

"But no one who's actually seen one?" Joe asked when she paused.

She winced. It was a sore point, she had to admit. "No."

"And then you saw my picture in that article last year?"

"Yes." She perked up as she remembered her excitement that day. "I'd been working on a montage of photos from the old monarchy, and I'd gotten so familiar with the faces. When I saw yours, it was like a bolt of lightning hit me. I just knew."

"Whoa. Not so fast." He held up a hand as though he were stopping a train. "You still don't really know anything."

"But I strongly suspect. Don't you?"

He didn't seem happy with that question. "I don't know," he muttered.

"There are ways to find out."

He looked uncomfortable and turned his gaze out toward the ocean.

"What if I don't want to find out?" he asked softly, then he swung back and faced her. "Tell me, how is being one of these royal guys who everyone wants to kill going to enhance my life?"

CHAPTER EIGHT

KELLY BLINKED AT Joe. This was quite a revelation. It had never occurred to her that anyone would want to pass up a chance to be a prince, especially of Ambria. It was an honor. Why didn't he get that?

"Do it for history," she suggested.

"For history?" He raised one eyebrow and looked amused.

"Why not? What have you done for history lately?"

He thought about that for a few seconds, and then started to laugh. "What's history done for me?" he countered.

"We don't know yet." She hesitated, then admitted, "Let's put it this way. In all honesty, if you are one of them, it could do a lot for me."

He nodded. "Your reputation?"

"Yes. I'd finally get a little respect at the agency."

He smiled, admiring the light of ambition in her eyes. She had spirit. He liked a woman with spirit. "Does your work mean that much to you?"

"Sure."

The sound of Mei's voice cut off anything else she

might have been about to say. Once Kelly knew the baby was awake, that was her first priority.

"Want to come help me change her?" she asked him hopefully.

He paused a moment, then shook his head. "I'll get dinner ready."

Disappointed, she went in by herself. Mei was standing at the crib railing and calling out, not crying yet, just letting people know she was ready to get out and join the world again. Kelly laughed and held out her arms. Mei threw out her own arms and laughed, too. Kelly held her tightly, murmuring loving words, and wished with all her heart that she would see this sort of interaction between Mei and her daddy soon. Very, very soon.

What they'd been doing so far wasn't working, and there wasn't much time left. She had to start training Mei to deal with Joe in a good, loving way. In another forty-eight hours, she wasn't going to be here for this little girl. Or for Joe, either.

Having Mei acting this way toward Joe complicated things as far as getting him to accept his place as a prince of Ambria. But in some ways, it was all part of the same challenge. Mei had to accept Joe, Joe had to accept his heritage. And what did Kelly have to accept? The fact that she was starting to fall for him in a big way?

No! Where had that thought come from? Nothing of the sort. She was okay. She'd be leaving soon. This was nothing but an assignment, even if she had assigned it to herself. It was a job she had to do. Falling for Joe was not part of the plan.

The main problem wasn't romance, however. The main problem was getting him to realize how important his position was. She had to back off, calm down and think this through. Why wasn't it working? Why wasn't he sharing her concerns? What was she doing wrong in the way she was presenting it to him? Most of all, why didn't he believe that he was the prince?

Quickly, she went back over what had happened since she'd come face-to-face with him. Of course, at first she'd assumed he knew. She'd never dreamed that he would think she was crazy when she brought up the subject. He had no idea who he really was, and at first he'd taken it as a joke.

But what had she really done to convince him? Why should he believe it? She hadn't presented any evidence to him. That was what was missing. She had to lay the foundation or it wasn't going to work.

Kelly changed Mei, played with her for a few minutes, then got her ready for her dinner. She brought her out and put her in the high chair, then got down a jar of baby food and a long plastic spoon. Meanwhile, she chatted with Joe, who was serving up a frozen lasagna he'd warmed in the oven. He'd also whipped up a couple of delicious salads to go with it.

"Hey," she said in admiration. "This looks great. You can cook for me anytime."

"Is that a promise?" he teased.

But when she met his gaze, she stopped smiling. There was something serious lurking behind his humor. What did it mean? She looked away again.

They sat down and ate, laughing companionably

together over things Mei did. The baby didn't seem to pay much attention to her father now, but at least she wasn't screaming every time he came near her.

"She's getting better, don't you think?" Joe asked hopefully, after he'd handed Mei a sippy cup of milk and she'd hesitated only a moment before taking it and drinking.

"Oh yes. I'm sure of it."

Kelly wasn't sure at all, but she wanted to keep his spirits up.

He looked at her and smiled, and she wondered if he could read her mind.

"So when do you think they'll invade?" Joe asked innocently as they leaned back from their meal.

"Who?" Kelly asked blankly.

"The nefarious Granvilli clan, of course. Tell me, what's their modus operandi? Do they like to sneak in at night when their targets are sleeping? Or do they prefer a full frontal confrontation in broad daylight?"

She groaned. "Now you're just making fun of me." Her eyes flashed. "You'll see. Something very bad will happen and then you'll find I was right."

He tossed down his napkin and laughed. "That's reassuring."

"Sorry," she said, rising to take Mei from her high chair. "I'm trying to be pragmatic and realistic. Too much optimism leaves you unprepared for whatever might be coming next."

Joe stayed where he was while she took Mei off to clean her up and change her. He wasn't sure what he thought about this royalty business. It seemed like a red herring to him. If Kelly wasn't so cute and fun to have around, he would be dismissing the whole thing out of hand. But the longer she helped him with Mei and the more she tried to get him to understand how important she thought this all was, the more he understood just how adorable and sweet *she* was, and the more he wanted to do whatever it took to make her happy. So here he sat, contemplating being a prince.

What the hell?

She came back, baby in tow, and he got up to clear the table and wash the dishes. She didn't say anything, but she had a portfolio with her and she took Mei into the living room. He knew she was up to something. He went on cleaning up from dinner, then went out to the living room to join her.

Kelly stood holding Mei on one hip. As he entered the room, she turned and gave him a tremulous smile. She'd arranged eight-by-ten-inch photographs in groups over every flat surface in the room.

"Meet the royal family," she told him with a flourish.

Joe stared at the pictures, and his heart began to beat faster.

"Where did you get these?" he asked her.

"This is my area of research. I brought them along to show to you."

Taking a deep breath, he began to walk the length of the room, looking at them all, one by one. His mouth was dry and he could tell his hands were shaking. He could tell right away that there was something about these people that he connected with, something familiar that resonated in the core of his being. These pictures were going to change his life.

"Well, what do you think?" Kelly asked, after he'd had a good long time to soak it all in.

He turned and looked at her with troubled eyes. "Tell me exactly who these people are," he said.

She pursed her lips. "I warn you, I'm going to talk about them as though they were your family."

He nodded impatiently. "Whatever. Let's just do this. Let's get it done."

She stopped before the first picture, of a very handsome couple dressed quite formally. "This is King Grandor and Queen Elineas, your father and your mother," she said quietly. "This is their official portrait."

She picked up two enlarged snapshots, one of them just after a tennis game, another of them sitting before a fire, both showing an engaging, happy pair. "And here are pictures of them in more casual settings."

He nodded again. His throat was too tight to speak.

"Here is your uncle Lord Gustav. Your uncle the Archduke Nathanilius—the one who just died. Your aunt, Lady Henrika. Your grandmother, also named Henrika."

Kelly paused, giving Joe time to take it all in. He went over each picture slowly as she named the subject, examining the eyes, studying the faces. She put Mei down in her play chair with all its attached toys and turned back to him. As she watched, she could see that his emotions were calming.

"Are you okay?" she asked him at last.

He looked up, his eyes hooded, as though he wasn't comfortable letting her see just how moving this was to him. "Yes. Why wouldn't I be?"

She shrugged. "For a minute there I thought you were freaking out."

He gave her a smile that was quickly gone. "Not me," he said, going on to the next. "Who are these charming children?"

"These are pictures of your sisters and a couple of your brothers. They were taken just a few weeks before the coup."

Joe lingered, studying each face as if trying to learn as much as he could about that individual. His expression had gone from shock and pure reaction to great interest. The pictures might even be said to be doing what she'd wanted them to.

She pointed to the last one. "And here is a picture of you as a four-year-old."

He stared at that one a long, long time. Did he see himself in it? She wasn't sure. She knew darn well *she* saw him in the adorable little blond boy playing with a pail and shovel in the sand.

Joe felt like a man riding a hang glider over a storm. A part of him was clinging hard to the reality that had been his all his life. The other part was catching a thrilling ride on a rainbow. Which one would he end up with? Was he even allowed to choose, or had these things already been chosen for him?

He'd grown up in a working-class family, learning working-class behavior. His goals had been those of the salt-of-the-earth types he saw around him. He'd always known he had a bright, inquiring mind that wanted to go a bit further than most of those around him cared to venture. He'd certainly taken enough ribbing for it in his past. But once he'd become an adult, he'd lived his own life and followed his own dreams. Still, they'd had nothing to do with royalty.

Royalty only happened in fairy tales. He wasn't a fairy-tale sort of guy. Everything in him wanted to reject this crazy idea. It just wasn't him.

And yet, as he looked at this picture of a little prince playing in the sand, something deep inside him resonated with it just a little. As he stared into the faces of the royals Kelly had put around the room, something in each one caught at a place in his emotional makeup that he wouldn't have dreamed of before she had dropped into his life. But he couldn't admit it to her, not yet.

Finally he looked up and smiled at her. "Thanks, Kelly," he said calmly. "This really does help me get a fix on what this is all about."

She waited, hoping to hear more, but he wasn't forthcoming so she shrugged and went on to the next subject.

"I called my office a few hours ago," she told him significantly. "There's news."

He frowned. "What sort of news?"

"There are rumors that one of your brothers has been sighted on his way to the funeral in Piasa."

Joe's mouth quirked. He didn't bother to remind her there was no proof that any of these were his brothers. Not yet. "Which one?"

"Prince Darius." She pointed to his picture. "He would be almost two years older than you."

Joe nodded, looking at the picture and frowning uncertainly. "More rumors," he murmured. "I'd like to hear some substantiated eyewitness reports."

"Of course. We all would." She searched his face. "So what do you think?" she asked again. "Does seeing these pictures stir any memories? Do you feel a connection to these people on any sort of visceral level?"

She was so eager, so hopeful. He turned away and didn't answer for a long time, gazing at the pictures of his brothers. Finally he gave her a lopsided smile.

"Sure, Kelly. They look like a great bunch. Who wouldn't want to be related to people like this?" Joe raked his fingers through his hair, making it stand up in crazy patches like it did right after surfing. "But just because they and their lifestyle of the time are very attractive, that doesn't mean anything, does it?"

"But what if you are related to them? Wouldn't that be wonderful?"

He gave her a glance that said *Not so fast*. "How can I ever know for sure?"

"DNA testing," she answered quickly. "It will take a while to get the results, but it will be worth it. You'll have the facts."

He stared at her for a long moment in a way that made her think he wasn't really seeing her at all. He was seeing something else—something in the past, something in his future.

"But do I really want them?" He looked tortured as he turned away. "Would knowing mean I would suddenly have a whole new area of responsibility? What would I have to do? And what the hell do I care, anyway?"

She swallowed, surprised and somewhat dismayed at his reaction. "Are you saying you really *don't* care? That you don't want to know?"

"Kelly…" He turned and stared at her again. Then his expression softened and he took her face in his hands and tilted it up. "Kelly, I know you care so much. You've been living with this, trying to get the answer to this puzzle, for so long. You have your own life invested in it. But I don't. Until I see more than this…"

She was breathless, not sure why he was holding her face this way, as though she was someone he treasured. But she liked it—she really liked it. Her body felt as though it were made of liquid, as if she could float away on a magical stream of happiness if she let herself. He was so close and his touch felt so good.

He seemed to be studying her face, but she hardly noticed. She was caught up in a wave of feeling—feeling his hands on her face, feeling his breath on her lips, feeling his affection, even his desire. Was that right? Wasn't that the flicker of something hot and raw that she saw in the depths of his eyes? Was she imagining it?

As if to answer that question, he dropped a quick, soft kiss on her lips, and then reluctantly—she could swear it was reluctantly—drew away.

"I've already got a life planned out, Kelly," he told her. "I don't need a major change. I'm not sure I could handle it."

Her face felt cool where his palms had been, and now her heart was chilled by what he was saying.

"I...I think you could handle just about anything," she said, working to regain her equilibrium. "I've seen you surf."

His quick flash of a grin reassured her, but he still looked as though he wanted to go. Maybe he needed to. Maybe he needed to assimilate the information he'd taken in here. Still, *she* needed more from *him*. She had only a short time left and she had to get all she could from it.

"Wait," she said, afraid he would leave the room entirely. "Please, Joe. Do one more thing for me."

He looked into her eyes with a tenderness that confused her. "Anything," he replied.

She took in a deep breath. "Sit down here on the couch with me for a few minutes. Tell me about what you remember of your childhood. Help me fill in some of the blanks."

"Sure." He shrugged, then glanced at Mei. "Is she going to last?"

Kelly hesitated. "I think so. She's still tired from her flight, I think. Baby jet lag. So she'll probably go down soon. But we'll hope for the best."

Kelly sat and so did he.

"The information I have on your background is really sketchy," she began. "I know you spent your early years in London. The woman listed as your mother died, and you were adopted by your aunt and uncle, and they brought you to New York. By the time you were a teenager, the family had moved here to San Diego."

He gazed at her in wonder. "How do you know all this stuff?"

She shrugged. "I know where to look. It's all in public records, and not that hard to get when you know what to ask for." She gave him a quick smile. "It's my job, remember?"

He began to look at her as though he wasn't sure if she was the same Kelly he thought he knew. "Are you some kind of private eye?"

"I've told you all about it before. I'm an analyst. An investigator of sorts. But really just an analyst."

He was still looking at her as though he wasn't too sure, but she was ready to move on.

"Listen, I know about your service with the Army Rangers in Southeast Asia. And I know a little bit about what you went through in the Philippines."

He glanced at her and bit his tongue. There were things he could say, but he wasn't going to say them. She might think she knew, but there was no way she could know the half of it.

"I know about how you were wounded. In fact, it was that article in a local newspaper I just happened to see, all about your wounds and how you were recuperating. That's how I first found out about you. What I don't know is all the connections in between. Tell me why you went into the army instead of going to college. Tell me how you ended up being adopted by those people." She put her hands out, palms up. "Tell me the story from your point of view."

He watched Mei playing with a stuffed clown for a moment, then took a deep breath. "Okay, here goes. Here's what the woman I called 'Mum' always told me."

"Your, uh, mother?"

"No. My mother was a maid who actually did work for the royal family of some country. Mum never seemed to be sure what one, but it could have been Ambria, I suppose. My mother's name was Sally Tanner. She wasn't married and no one knows who my father was. She brought me back to England when I was four, but she died when I was five. I actually remember her a bit. Just a little bit."

He paused for a moment, recalling it all. Yes, he remembered her. But he didn't remember loving her. And that had bothered him all his life.

"I got passed around from one relative to another for a few years and finally got adopted by a sister of Sally's. Martha and Ned Tanner. Martha is the one I called Mum. They brought me along when they emigrated to New York, and we moved to California when I was twelve."

"So you have a family," she noted, relieved to hear it.

He shrugged. "I *had* a family," he corrected. "A family of sorts. I never felt like I was any more than an afterthought, though. I never knew why they decided to adopt me. There was never any real closeness."

He stopped. What the hell was he doing, opening up old wounds to a woman he'd only just met? A woman he knew was fishing for exactly this type of information. Was he crazy? This was the sort of garbage that stirred up old resentments and made them fester. He never told anyone this stuff. Why was he telling her? He was going to stop. Let her find out what she wanted to know by going to these sources she seemed to be so good at finding.

Incredibly, despite his determination, he heard himself talking again. He was telling her more. Unbelievable.

"I grew up pretty much like any other American kid, playing baseball and football and living a typical suburban American life. Ned and Martha got divorced and things got a lot worse financially after that. My so-called brother and sister both began to get into trouble. Things just generally fell apart. So when I graduated high school, I wanted to get as far away from them all as possible. I joined the army. And I guess you know most of the rest."

She nodded, touched and saddened by what he'd gone through as a child. She was so sure he was royal, and yet he'd grown up in hard circumstances, the hardest being not having anyone to really love him. She wanted to put her arms around him and tell him it was okay, but she knew he wouldn't welcome something like that. Besides, what could she promise him? That life would be better from now on? That was something she really couldn't manipulate for him. Better to keep quiet.

By now, Mei was fussing and needed attention. Kelly rose, put a hand on his shoulder and said softly, "Thank you for telling me that, Joe. I know it's an intrusion to even ask you, so I really do appreciate it."

He caught her hand and brought it to his lips, kissing the palm in a way that startled her.

"Isn't it obvious I'll do just about anything for you?" he said, pretending to be teasing, but coming across as serious as she'd ever seen him. He let her go tend to the baby, but her heart was thumping.

She'd spent a lifetime finding all the men she met and dated completely inadequate. And now she'd turned around and fallen in love with a prince.

Mei, who had been so good for the last two days, fell apart when Kelly took her to her room. She cried and she wailed and she sobbed, and nothing could console her. Kelly rocked her and walked her and tried every trick she'd seen her sister-in-law employ. Nothing worked.

Joe looked in on them. "Anything I can do?" he asked.

Kelly shook her head. "She's just so tired, but she can't fall asleep," she told him. "I may have to put her down and let her cry herself to sleep, but I hate to do it. That can take hours."

He groaned. "Oh, well. You're a better man than I am, Gunga Din," he said as he walked back to the other room.

Kelly wasn't sure what that meant, but she knew it was a compliment, so took it in good spirits. But she was getting desperate as far as this baby was concerned.

She held Mei and rocked her and hummed a tune or two, trying to think of something she could sing besides "Rock-a-bye Baby," which she'd already done to death.

And suddenly one came to her. She hummed it for a moment and then began to sing. It was in a foreign tongue, but the words came naturally to her, and she realized after a moment that it was in Ambrian.

She didn't remember ever singing this song before, and yet she seemed to know all the words. She sang it more softly, again and again, and Mei finally began to quiet. It was the only thing that seemed to please the child. In a few minutes, she was asleep.

Kelly kept singing. She knew how easily babies came awake again and she was going to make sure this one was out. At the same time, she was marveling at the mind's ability to pull things from the past, things one didn't even know one possessed. She was singing a song in Ambrian that she was sure her mother must have sung to her when she was a baby. It was all there, sounds more than words, but nevertheless, complete. It felt like a miracle.

Joe heard the whole thing. He sat in the living room and listened to Kelly singing a song in a language he didn't understand, and suddenly he found he had tears streaming down his cheeks. He knew that song. Not consciously, not overtly, but his heart knew it. His soul had been nurtured by it years ago. It was a part of his heritage. He could never lose it.

And now he knew the truth. He was Ambrian. There was no denying it any longer.

CHAPTER NINE

RISING SLOWLY FROM his chair, Joe went to the garage and rummaged around until he found his old army duffel bag. Deep inside, down at the bottom, he found an old cigar box wrapped in rubber bands, and pulled it out. Most of the bands disintegrated as he tried to remove them, and the box opened easily. Inside were artifacts of a life he didn't really remember, and a place he didn't really know. He'd never understood what they were. Maybe Kelly would be able to interpret them for him. He tucked the box under his arm and went back into the house.

She had just put Mei down and was coming out of the room when she met Joe in the hall. He showed her the box.

"Come on into the living room. I want you to take a look at this," he said.

He spread the items out on the coffee table, under the light, and the two of them looked at them. Kelly's heart was beating out of her chest. There were three gold buttons with lion heads carved in them, such as might have been on a little boy's dress jacket. There was a small child's prayer book, a small signet ring, and a brightly colored ribbon with a tin medal dangling from it.

Kelly picked up the prayer book. There was an inscription in the front, written in Ambrian. She wasn't great at the language, but she knew enough to translate, "To my most adorable little son. Say your prayers! Your Mama."

Kelly could hardly breathe. She looked at Joe. "Where did you get these things?"

He shook his head. "I don't know. I've always had them. I assumed my mother, Sally Tanner, had collected them for me. I've never really paid any attention to them. I'm not sure why I've even kept them."

Kelly nodded, her eyes shining. "You understand what this means, don't you?"

He groaned and tipped his head back. "Probably."

"You are almost certainly…" she swallowed hard and forced herself to say it "…Prince Cassius."

"But what if I don't want to be?" he asked.

"Joe…"

He put up a hand to stop her and give himself space to explain his current thinking. "What I'm going to say now may sound like blasphemy to you. I'm a simple guy. I was raised by simple people. I've lived a simple life."

She was shaking her head. "I don't think what you've done with your life is simple at all."

"But it's not an upper-class, royal life. Kelly, once you get to my age, I don't think there's any turning back. I am what I am and what I'll always be."

She pressed her lips together, thinking. She understood

his argument, but didn't believe it was valid, and she was trying to figure out how to counter it successfully.

"I think you have a skewed idea of what royalty is really like," she said at last. "As people, they're not necessarily all that special. These days a lot of them seem pretty much like everyone else."

Joe made a face. "You mean like that prince of that little country I saw on the news the other day—the one who photographers caught with about twenty naked ladies running around on his yacht with him?"

Kelly laughed. "Those were not ladies."

"Probably not." He rubbed his head and grimaced. "Now, I'm not going to claim that such a thing wouldn't appeal to the male animal in me, but they said this prince had a wife and a baby at home. What normal man would think it was okay to do that?"

She sighed. "Sure, there are some royalty who take advantage of their opportunities in a rotten way. But there are plenty that don't."

"Name one."

She hesitated. "I don't have to name one," she said evasively. "And anyway, if there weren't any, you could be the first." Her smile was triumphant. "You haven't grown up being overindulged. You've got your own brand of honesty and integrity. You won't go bad."

His own smile was crooked but his eyes were still sad. "Your faith in me is touching," he said.

"Why not? You deserve it." She picked up the little gold buttons. "I'll bet these were on the jacket you wore the night you escaped."

He gave her a startled look. "What makes you so sure I escaped?"

She put them down and sat back. "Okay, here's what I see as what probably happened—based on a lot of research I've done on the subject and a lot of memoirs I've read. The castle was attacked. Your parents had already set up an elaborate set of instructions to certain servants, each of whom was assigned a different royal child, to smuggle you out if the worst happened."

"And you know this how?"

She shrugged. "People who knew about it wrote explanations later. Anyway, the worst did happen. The Granvillis began to burn the castle. Your mother's favorite lady-in-waiting was supposed to take care of you—she wrote about that in her book on the coup. But something went wrong and you ended up being whisked away by one of the kitchen maids instead, an English girl named Sally Tanner. Here's what I think happened after that. Sally catches a ride to the mainland in a rowboat. The trip takes most of the night, and it becomes impossible to hide you from the others escaping as well. She doesn't want them to know you are one of the royals, so she claims you as her own secret love child, and as no one else on the boat actually knows her, this is accepted."

His face was white. She stopped. "Joe, what is it?"

"I remember that boat ride," he said hoarsely. "The feeling of terror on that trip has stayed with me ever since."

Reaching out, she took his hand in hers. "Now Sally has you and doesn't know what to do with you. She

didn't get the special instructions the others are following. She just grabbed a kid she saw needed help, and
saved him. Now what?"

Joe laced fingers with Kelly's. "This is all sounding
so right to me," he told her. "I can't believe you know
this much."

"It's partly speculation, but speculation built on facts,"
she said. "Anyway, she doesn't know what to do. Should
she try to contact someone? But that might be certain
death for you. She knows, by now, what happened to
your parents. She can't see any alternative. She might
as well take you with her and hope something happens
that makes it possible to find out what to do with you.
She takes you to London to stay with her family, who
aren't really sure who you are or what to make of you.
They suspect you really are Sally's, a secret child she
hadn't told them about. She tells them your name is Joe.
Before Sally can contact anyone to find out what to do
with you, she dies in an accident."

He nodded. "And that's why they tell me she's my
mother." His half smile was sad. "And that's why I can't
remember loving her the way a son should. When she
died, I was probably still waiting for my real mom to
show up and take me home."

"There you go."

He sat brooding for a few minutes. Kelly was still
holding his hand, and she smiled at him.

"Joe, I'm sure this is all hard to hear, but you needed
to know. Not only so you can decide if you want to take
your rightful place in Ambrian society, but also so you
can protect yourself. You need to be careful of people

like Sonja. Or anyone who might come from the current regime."

He frowned, still trying to assimilate it all. "Tell me again what is so bad about the current regime?"

"They killed your parents."

His eyebrows rose. "There is that." He thought of those beautiful people in the photographs. To think of his parents as a king and queen still seemed utterly ridiculous. But that couple had looked right to him. He liked them. He had to admit there was a crack in his heart when he thought of what might have been—if only the coup hadn't happened.

Joe looked at Kelly, enjoying the way her blonde curls were rioting around her pretty face. She was so gracious and decent and caring. And basically happy. How was he going to make sure that Mei turned out that way?

"Kelly, you said something earlier about some bad things that had happened in your life. I feel like I'm hogging all the emotion around here. Let's hear your story."

"Oh gosh, it was nothing like what happened to you. I'm embarrassed to even bring it up. It's nothing at all. It's just everyday life disappointments. You know how that is...."

"Come on." He tugged on her hand. "I told you about myself. Your turn. Don't hold out on me."

"Joe..."

"You told me about your family, and that there was a time when you were all very close."

"Yes." She went still. "That's true. Actually, I had a wonderful childhood. I tend to forget that sometimes."

"You see, that's what I want for Mei. Somehow I want to create that warm, safe, nurturing ideal, like the Norman Rockwell pictures, for her. Everything's got to be perfect."

Unspoken were the words *like I never had* and she heard them loud and clear. She often felt the same way.

"So come on. What about your family?"

"What about it? I've had one. It's pretty much gone now."

Funny, but this was an area where they had some things in common. No real family around. Not anymore.

"But your brothers and those nieces and nephews."

She nodded. "I see them at Thanksgiving and Christmas. The rest of the year they forget I exist."

Joe looked surprised and somewhat shocked. "Kelly, I didn't realize…"

"Oh, I don't mean to sound bitter. Really. But they're young professionals with young families, and they have very full lives, lives I don't fit into very easily."

He looked puzzled. "What happened to your parents?"

"My mother died when I was eighteen. When she was alive, I definitely had a family. She was the glue that kept us all together. And she was my biggest booster, my best friend. So her death was a major blow to me. It really threw me for a loop for months." And it still gave her a horrible, hollow feeling in the pit of her stomach whenever she thought of it.

"And your father?"

"My father." She took a deep breath and thought about him. A tall, handsome man with distinguished gray hair at his temples, he'd been a prime target for hungry females of a certain age as soon as her mother had died. They'd swarmed around him like bees, and he didn't last long. Kelly remembered with chagrin how she'd vowed to dedicate her life to taking care of the man, only to turn around and find him carrying on with a woman in tight T-shirts and short shorts, the sort of floozy her mother wouldn't have given the time of day to.

"My sixty-five-year-old father married a woman in her late thirties who wanted to pretend I didn't exist," she said, not even trying to hide the bitterness she felt this time. "They live in Florida. I never see them."

"Wow. I'm sorry."

He was looking at her as though he wasn't sure who she was. From the beginning, she'd fit his image of the perfect daughter in the perfect family full of people who loved each other and made sure things went right. Lots of presents at birthdays. A huge turkey at Thanksgiving. All the things he'd never had. And now to find out she was as lonely as he was… What a revelation. Joe had a hard time dealing with it.

Where, after all, was happiness in the world? Maybe you just had to make your own.

"So you see, we're alike," she said with a wistful smile. "We both had great families, and then we blew it."

"We didn't blow it," he countered. "Somebody blew it for us."

"Regardless, it was blown."

"So that's the goal," he said, holding her hand in his and moving in closer. "Don't blow it for the next generation."

She smiled at him. He was going to kiss her soon and she was ready for it. In fact, she could hardly wait. "You got it."

"We need to concentrate on finding good people to marry," he said, his brow furrowed as he thought about this. At the same time, he was cupping her cheek with his hand and studying her lips. Anticipation—what a sweet thing it was.

She nodded, feeling breathless. "Of course, that won't be any problem for you," she noted drily.

"What are you talking about?" he asked as he widened his hand and raked his fingers into the hair behind her head, taking her into his temporary possession.

She made a sound of derision. "You are the type of beautiful man that women swoon over all the time," she said, swooning a little bit herself.

He frowned. "So?" He pulled her closer.

She pushed his hand away. "I refuse to swoon," she claimed, but her words were a little slurred. His attentions were already having their effect.

A smile began to form in his eyes. "So you're an anti-swooner, huh?"

"You could say that. I'm anti feeding your oversize ego any more than absolutely necessary."

He dropped a soft kiss on her lips, then drew back so that he could look at her. "At least you admit my ego deserves a bit of nutrition."

"Hah!" She rolled her eyes. "Not really. I think it needs a strict diet." She smiled, checking out his reaction. "And maybe a few hard truths to help it get over itself."

"Hard truths, huh?" He began to pull her into his arms. "And you're just the person to give them to me. Right?"

She pretended to be challenging him at every turn. "Why not?"

He gave her that helpless look he put on when he was teasing. "Can I help it if women love me?"

"Yes." Kelly tried to pull out of his embrace and failed miserably. "Yes, you can. You cannot be quite so accessible. You walk around so free and easy with that lascivious grin...."

He stopped and looked thoroughly insulted. "What lascivious grin?"

"The one you've got on." She tapped his lips with her forefinger. "Right there on your face."

"You mean this one?" He leaned over her, finding the way to her mouth and kissing her with passion and conviction. "See?" he murmured against her cheek. "Women can't help but kiss me."

Kelly didn't answer. She was too busy doing exactly that.

The morning dawned brilliantly. The sun was shining in glorious celebration and the ocean gleamed like a trove of diamonds. They ate breakfast on the deck, watching the day begin. Joe had made a trayful of scrambled eggs and a pile of English muffins and honey, and Kelly fed

Mei from a small jar of baby oatmeal, then gave her some of the eggs as well. They talked and laughed as the seagulls swooped around, hoping for a handout. Kelly couldn't remember a more wonderful breakfast at any time in her life. This was the best.

A little later, after changing Mei and cleaning up from breakfast, she carried the baby out to find Joe sitting on the deck, looking a bit forlorn.

He'd decided to ignore all this royalty talk for now. He needed time to let it sink in. Today, he was all about Mei and doing what he could to change her mind about him.

"Hi," Kelly said. "What are you doing?"

"Sitting here feeling sorry for myself."

Reality was a bummer. He thought back to the dreams he used to have about what it was going to be like once Mei arrived. Father and daughter. He was already running little clips in his head of himself teaching her how to throw a ball. When he explained that to Kelly, she laughed at him.

"She's a girl. She might not be into sports."

"What are you, some kind of chauvinist?"

"No." Kelly looked lovingly into Mei's small cute face. "What about it, little girl? Want to play ball? Or take ballet lessons?"

Joe shook his head, enjoying how the two of them interacted. Mei was such a darling child. If only she liked him.

"Whatever she wants to do, we'll do," he said firmly. "She's in the driver's seat on that one. It's just that..." He sighed. It didn't pay to get your hopes up.

"I've got an idea," he said, smiling at Mei, who studiously looked away without reciprocating. "I want to take her on a boat ride before the nanny gets here this afternoon."

"You think she's ready for that?" Kelly asked anxiously.

"Sure. There are some boats that go out from the pier. Just small, one hour trips. I think she'll like it."

Actually, it sounded like fun. "Let's go," Kelly said.

A few preparations had to be made. Joe went out shopping to find a little sweat suit for Mei, as her supplies from the Philippines had included nothing for cool weather.

"It will get cold out there on the bay, and this way we'll know she's warm as toast," Joe explained.

Kelly had to admit he was thinking ahead better than she was.

As they stood in line at the dock, Kelly noticed their reflection in the glass at the ticket office. They looked like a beautiful family. It warmed her heart, until she stopped herself.

Now, why had she thought that? What a crazy idea. They could never be a family. Joe was a true image of the prince she was convinced he was, and Mei looked like a little princess. But Kelly looked like an ordinary person. A nice, fairly pretty, ordinary person. There wasn't a hint of royalty in her demeanor.

The boat ride started out well. The captain was full of odd stories and funny anecdotes, and he kept up a running dialogue that had them in stitches half the time.

He showed them where huge sea lions had taken over a small boat dock, yelling like crazy when anyone came near. Then he drove on to an area where sea otters infested a kelp bed, some lying on their backs and opening oysters against rocks held on their bellies. There was a seabird rookery and an island made of an old buoy and a lot of barnacles that housed a family of pelicans. And then they headed toward open sea to find dolphins and possibly a whale or two.

They caught sight of a dolphin scampering through the water, but were out of luck with the whales, despite the fact that Kelly kept urging Mei to "look for whales, sweetie. Keep looking!"

Mei looked very hard, but there was no sign of a whale. She seemed disappointed, so it was time for Joe to pull out his surprise.

He'd gone into the shop at the dock and picked up a present for her, and now he took it from his jacket pocket and held it out. It was a stuffed killer whale, just the right size for a toddler.

"Here you are, honey," he said to his beloved daughter. "I bought you a present. Here's your whale."

Mei looked at him and looked at the whale, then held out her hand to take it. He gave it to her, and without a second of hesitation, she threw it overboard, right into the water. It tumbled in the wake for a second or two, then sank like a stone.

They sat for a moment, staring after it, stunned. Kelly couldn't believe Mei had actually done that. This was too much, a step too far. It couldn't be allowed. To overlook such shenanigans would be no good for Mei, and criminal toward Joe. Kelly glanced at the child, who looked pleased as punch.

"Mei," she said tersely, "No! Your daddy gave you that whale as a gift. You don't treat people that way. You don't throw away presents that people give you out of love."

Joe felt as though someone had just hit him in the head with a brick. It was no use. None of this was going to work. His little girl hated him. In a way, it almost felt as though a small part of Angie had just rejected him for good. How did he come back from that one? What more could he do about it? He really didn't have a clue.

All this garbage about being a prince didn't mean a thing to him. All he really wanted was for his little girl to accept him. Was that never going to happen?

"Mei, you hurt your daddy's feelings," Kelly was saying, keeping her voice calm but firm. "Tell your daddy that you're sorry."

Kelly knew very well that Mei couldn't even say the word *sorry,* but she wanted to get the emotional injury through to her at least. The concept was in that little brain, somewhere. She just wanted Mei to know that people had taken notice.

Mei's huge dark eyes were unreadable, but Kelly could tell her strong words were having an effect, so she stopped. She didn't want to overwhelm her with emotions. Pulling her close, she hugged her tightly and whispered in her ear, "Daddy loves you. And you love your daddy. You just don't know it yet."

The walk home wasn't as filled with fun as the walk to the pier had been, but they returned in time to greet the new nanny. Mrs. Gomez was a warm and lovely older woman, and Kelly could tell right away she was going to work out fine. It was a relief to have someone else to help with the burden of caring for Mei every day. That couldn't go on forever. But for now, it was the way things had to be.

Once Kelly had met Mrs. Gomez, she had no more doubts about her possibly being a spy sent by Sonja. The woman was an open book, a wonderful lady who loved children. But after a couple of hours, Kelly began to wonder what her own purpose here was.

She said as much to Joe. "I guess I could go back to my hotel," she offered, as she helped him wash dishes after lunch.

He looked at her in horror. "What are you talking about?

"I...well, with Mrs. Gomez here, I thought..."

It hit him like a thunderbolt—Kelly might leave. For some reason he'd just assumed she was going to be around as long as he needed her. That was foolish, wasn't it?

He frowned, his gaze traveling over every inch of her, really seeing her, really feeling how empty it would be around here without her. He liked her. He liked her a lot. Maybe too much.

Now why would he think a thing like that? Because of Angie?

He waited a second or two for the pain to grip his heart. There it was, but not quite as sharp as usual. And not quite as anguished.

He turned away, disturbed. A tiny thread of panic

hit him for a moment. Was he losing his feelings about Angie? Were they going to fade?

He remembered when they had racked him with such torture he'd almost thought about ending it all. Life hadn't seemed worth living without her. He didn't think he could go on with such pain wrapped around him like a straitjacket. And then, little by little, the pain had become a part of him.

Was it going to fade if he let himself fall for Kelly? Without it, would he still be the man he thought he was?

He looked at her again and knew it didn't matter. He liked her. He wanted her around. She made him happy in a totally different way than Angie had. But happy was happy. He didn't want Kelly to leave.

"You thought you wouldn't have anything to do here?" he challenged with a smile. "You're nuts." He gave a one-shouldered shrug. "There's always me to satisfy."

She couldn't keep from smiling at that one. "You want me to stay?"

"Heck, yes."

"Are you sure?"

He turned and held her by the shoulders. "Let's put it this way—you're not going anywhere."

She shivered with a feeling very close to delight. His hands felt warm and protective, and he was leaning closer, looking at her mouth. He just might kiss her.

"I'm going somewhere on Saturday," she reminded him. "I have to go home."

"Not if we think of a way to keep you here," he said

huskily, and his mouth took hers gently, and then with more urgency, kissing her again and again, until her lips parted and she invited him in. His arms came around her and she arched into his embrace.

"Kelly, Kelly," he murmured against her ear. "You've got to stay. I can't do without you."

Mrs. Gomez was coming down the hall with Mei, and they pulled apart, but Kelly carried the warmth of his words and the thrill of his kiss with her for the rest of the afternoon. It didn't mean a thing, she knew, but it sure was nice. While it lasted.

Despite the teasing and the kissing, it was quite evident that Joe was troubled by all the changes in his life. When he announced he was taking some time off to go surfing, Kelly knew he really needed space alone to think. She watched him walk away in his cutoff shorts, with his board under his arm and his wet suit over his shoulder and sighed. He was so gorgeous. But he had so much on his mind, and she hoped he found some peace in the cold California waters.

She called her office to see if there was any news, or if Jim had found out anything about Sonja Smith. She hadn't expected much on that score, and sure enough, he hadn't found anything.

"I did find that there are a number of small enclaves of Ambrian exiles we didn't have in the database before, all centered around the San Diego area. So she is probably a member of one of those."

"But you don't know much about them."

"Nope. Still working on that."

"Okay, Jim. Here goes. I got a pretty good confirmation. Joe is almost certainly Prince Cassius."

"So you think he's the real deal."

"Yes, I do."

"Only DNA testing can prove it. Is he willing?"

"He will be. Can you work on getting him a liaison to the current wise men involved? I think someone ought to contact him about going to the funeral."

"You got it. I know who to call."

"Thanks."

"Shall I have him phone you?"

She sighed. "No. I won't be here much longer. Better call Joe directly."

"Okay. And Kelly?"

"Yes?"

"Good work."

She smiled. "Thanks, Jim." And as she hung up she realized he hadn't made one joke at her expense.

CHAPTER TEN

KELLY TOOK MEI down to the strand where the best surfing was, looking for Joe. They found him just as he was coming out of the water. He was wearing his wet suit now and at first Mei looked at this monster in black neoprene coming toward them in horror. When he got close she realized who it was, and Kelly noticed that although she didn't react in a friendly manner, she wasn't stiff with resentment as she'd been before. And when he shook his head, spraying water all over her, Mei actually laughed and clapped her hands together. And then she turned away when he smiled at her.

Joe didn't care right now. The moment was too good to let little things spoil it. He'd had a good workout and thought some things through, and he'd seen his two favorite women in the world standing in the sand, waiting for him as he came out of the ocean.

Good times. His heart was full.

They walked back to the house, enjoying the afternoon sun as it slanted against the neighborhood windows. It wasn't until they were back at the house that Joe told her he was going out in a half hour.

"I've got an appointment, believe it or not. I need a shower and then I'll be gone for about an hour or so."

"Oh," she said. "Okay. Well, I have some things to do. I guess I'll see you later."

He looked at her quizzically. "So you're not going to ask me who the appointment is with?" he teased, as she started to turn away.

She gazed at him, wide eyed. "It's really none of my business. But if you want to tell me…"

He shook his head and waved his hand dismissively. "No, not really. It'll just get you all riled up."

Now, of course, she had to know.

"Okay, Joe. You're dying to tell me. So tell me already. Who's your appointment with?"

He grinned at her. "Sonja. I'm meeting her at the coffee place."

Kelly put one hand on her hip and glared at him. "What?"

"I saw her this morning when I went to the Baby Boutique to find the sweatsuit for Mei. She wants to go over some of her ideas with me."

"What sort of ideas?" Kelly asked suspiciously.

"I guess I'll find out when we meet," he said cheerfully. "I'd ask you to come along, but something tells me we wouldn't get much accomplished that way."

He was right about that. Kelly fumed a bit, then told him, "Joe, you have to be very careful what you say around her. I really think she could be trouble."

"Really?"

"Don't let your guard down. And especially don't tell her about last night."

He pretended to look innocent. "You mean about how you were all over me on the couch?" he said, looking dreamy. "Frankly, I don't think she'd be interested."

"No, you know what I mean. About the things from your childhood. About our new determination about you. Things like that. It would be better if she didn't know."

He nodded, basically agreeing with her. "Despite the way I kid around, Kelly, I do understand where you're coming from. I'll be careful."

"I wish you wouldn't go at all," she fretted as the time came. "What if she—?"

"Hush." Joe put a finger to her lips. "I'll be back in an hour. You stay here and keep the home fires burning. Okay?"

Joe left for the coffee shop and Kelly began to pace. Every "what if?" possible was tumbling through her brain. Sonja was up to something. Kelly didn't trust her an inch. Why was he so easily taken in by her flirtatious act? He thought he was invincible, didn't he? He was going to get blindsided. If only Kelly was there to help him!

That was it. She *had* to be there to help him. Why hadn't she thought of that before? But she couldn't just walk in and stomp up to their table and flop down and join them. Though it would be fun to start needling Sonja, that wouldn't work out well.

No. She had to go incognito.

Racing to the room where she was storing her clothes, she pulled out the baggy sweatpants and hoodie sweatshirt she'd worn the day she first came face-to-face with Joe. It was the only disguise she had, so it would have to do. She asked Mrs. Gomez to listen for Mei, who was taking her nap, and she set off for the coffee shop.

She saw them right away, but they didn't even look up, so she wasn't afraid of being spotted. She ordered her drink, then took a table on the other side of the room and slipped into the chair, keeping her hood down over her eyes.

She could see them quite well, but couldn't hear a word. They were talking animatedly. Sonja seemed to be trying to convince him of something. He was shaking his head and generally doing what Joe did best—resisting joining in with female plans.

Sonja begged. Sonja pleaded. Sonja flirted and tried to persuade. Her body language told it all. And Joe deflected every bit of her proposal with humor and a shrug.

Which was all very well. But what else did Sonja have on her agenda for later? What was she planning to do to Joe? That was what was worrying Kelly.

For a moment, he seemed to get angry. He was making his own points rather forcefully. Kelly strained her ears, but she still couldn't hear a thing.

Then Sonja grabbed his hand and leaned toward him, pleading for something. Joe was looking long-suffering. He shifted away from Sonja. She leaned in closer. He turned his head away—and his eyes met Kelly's. He went completely still.

It was as though an electric charge ignited the air

between them. Kelly glanced around quickly, sure others must have seen it. He stared at her and she stared back. And slowly, a grin began to spread across his handsome face.

What was he going to do? She tensed, ready to run if she had to. He was still talking to Sonja, but he was looking at Kelly. In fact, he was making faces at her! She pretended to sip on the straw in her frappuccino, but her cheeks were flaming, she knew. No matter how much she pulled her hoodie down, she couldn't cover that up.

Finally Joe seemed to tell one too many jokes, and Sonja got up and left in a huff, leaving him behind at the table. He rose slowly and walked across the room to where Kelly was sitting, stopping at her table and waiting. Finally she couldn't stand it anymore and looked up into his face.

"What do you think you're doing here?" he demanded.

"I...I came to get a drink, of course." She straightened and tried to look cool, calm and collected. But he didn't buy it for a moment.

"Kelly."

"Well, I had to make sure. I don't trust her and I kept thinking about all the horrible things she might do."

"Uh-huh." He sank down into the chair across the table. "You thought she might get me into a hammerlock and force me into her car?"

Kelly pretended to consider it. "She's a big lady," she pointed out.

"Kelly." Reaching out, he took her hand in his.

"Listen, I think you take these people much too lightly," she told him earnestly. "They're dangerous." She searched his eyes. "So what did she do? Did she try to find out if you *are* Prince Cassius?"

"Yes. She did."

"I knew it!"

"Actually, she and Dory had pretty much decided I must be one of the princes, but they didn't know which one. They made the association from pictures just like you did."

Kelly snapped her fingers and murmured, "Shazam," under her breath.

"But she's not trying to get me to go back and sign up for my patriotic duty like you are. She wants me to help her make money. In fact, she offered me a job, paying twice as much if I really could prove I was the prince."

Kelly's mouth dropped open in reluctant admiration. "Oh, wow. Good move on her part."

"Yes, I thought so. Clever way to get me to confess." He grinned. "And nonviolent."

Kelly made a face at him. "You can never be too careful," she reminded him.

"Did you really think you were going to defend me from harm?" he asked, with laughter in his eyes and in his voice. "What were you going to do if she started to threaten me?"

"I assumed she really wouldn't do anything like that, at least not in public. But if she had a weapon…"

"You were prepared to throw yourself in front of me? Guard my life with your body?"

Kelly shook her head, all sweet innocence. "Whatever it takes."

"Hmm." He pursed his lips. "What about seduction?"

She frowned. "What about it?"

"If she'd tried it, would you be ready to guard me from that, too?"

She met his gaze and couldn't help but smile. "Maybe."

He held both her hands in his and looked at her across the table with so much affection she had to turn away.

"Don't worry, Kelly. I'll always be true. True to you."

That made her heart turn over in her chest. He might even mean that in the moment. But he didn't mean it the way she wished he would.

"Oh, Joe, stop it."

"You don't think I'm serious?"

She looked at him, loving him, regretting him. Didn't he get it yet? He was no longer free to decide whom he wanted to be true to. He was a prince of the realm. All his romances now belonged to the royal order. He didn't get to pick and choose.

Joe thought he was still in charge of his own destiny. He was a tough guy used to making his own decisions, fighting his own wars, making his own compromises when he chose to. He thought he could decide whether to go along with this royal gig or not, as his mood dictated. He was wrong.

And in some ways, it was all her fault. If she'd left him alone...

But no. That wouldn't have saved him. The Sonjas of the world were already seeking him out. If Kelly hadn't found him, someone else would have. The best, safest path would be for him to join his brothers and be a part of the fight for his homeland. She was convinced of that. Joe was going to have to come to that conclusion himself, though.

"Come on," she said to him, smiling with tears in her eyes. "Let's go back."

Mrs. Gomez went home at six in the evening, but first she made them a set of delicious quesadillas and a huge green salad to go with it. They had an intimate dinner after she left, talking softly, laughing a lot. Mei woke as they finished up, and Kelly brought her out and put her in the high chair to eat while Joe cleaned up the dishes.

He was thinking while he worked, remembering what Kelly had done for him the night before, with the pictures of the royal family, and it gave him an idea. He finished up and went to his room, opening a drawer where he kept most of his pictures of Angie. Just seeing her beloved face again made him smile, and that stopped him in his tracks. A smile instead of agony? Maybe things really were changing.

He took the pictures with him to the living room and invited Kelly to bring Mei to join him.

"What's up?" she asked curiously.

"I'm going to try it your way," he said. "I'm going to tell her about how I met her mother."

Kelly's dark eyes widened. "Oh, Joe," she said, and

a smile brightened her face. "I'll bring her in right away."

Joe set up pictures all around the room, and when Kelly came in, she put Mei down to play, and came over to sit by Joe on the couch. Joe looked at the little girl and felt his heart swell. He loved her so much and he was desperate to have at least a bit of that love returned.

"Mei, I want you to listen to me," he began, hoping this wasn't all for nothing. He was trying to keep his voice low and pleasant so as not to put her off, but so far, he might as well have been speaking pig latin. She made no sign that she heard a thing. This wasn't going to be easy.

"I'm not sure why you decided you had to make me pay like this. I think it probably has something to do with the fact that it was my fault you don't have your mother. I don't know how you could know that on a conscious level, but you feel it. Somehow, you feel it. And I accept it. I can't bring your mother back in the flesh. But I'm going to do as much as I can to show you what she was like. And how much she loved you. How much she still loves you. And how you came to be."

He rose from the couch and began to hold up photographs so that Mei might notice.

"These are pictures of your mother, Angie."

Mei seemed to be playing with her ring of plastic keys and completely ignoring everything Joe was saying and doing, but that didn't stop him. He began putting the pictures of Angie in more prominent places, not laying them on flat surfaces as Kelly had with the royals, but propping them up where Mei couldn't help but see them anytime she looked up from her toys.

"Here is the way your mother looked when I first met her. And now I'll tell you all about that."

He paused, and Mei glanced up as though she couldn't help herself. Joe smiled. Mei looked away quickly, but he met Kelly's gaze and they shared a grin. Mei could pretend all she wanted, but it was clear she was listening. How much she understood was another story, but at least she seemed to have some sense of what was going on here.

"I met Angie at a fiesta," he said softly. "I was stationed in the Philippines. We were out doing some cleanup work about a day's ride from Manila."

He held up some pictures and Kelly nodded. She was so impressed with Joe, so glad he'd decided to try this, although it didn't seem to be having much effect yet. So impressed that he could take advice, change his mind, do something because it might work. He was adaptable. You had to admire that in a guy.

Leaning forward, she asked, "By 'cleanup,' I assume you mean taking care of the bad guys?"

He favored her with a lopsided grin. "You catch on fast." He showed her a picture of himself and some of his army buddies riding in a Jeep. "Anyway, it was one of those huge Philippines parties that last for days. Everybody comes. There's singing and dancing and karaoke. And food—tables set up everywhere overflowing with food. Pancit and lumpia and roast pig."

Mei looked up at the familiar words. Joe smiled at her. She quickly looked down again.

"I caught sight of her right away. She was wearing a long skirt and a Philippines blouse with those high starched, gauzy sleeves. She looked like a butterfly about to take off over the trees. So pretty." He sighed. "Her mother didn't like me from the start. But Angie did, and for the moment, that was all that mattered. We got married and everyone had a wonderful time at our wedding. We didn't have a lot of time together, though. I had to go back to Manila and then, suddenly, I got shipped out to Thailand. She had you, Mei, while I was gone. By the time I finally got back there, rebels had taken over the whole area, killing most of the men."

Kelly gave a start, glancing at Mei. "Joe, do you really think you should…"

He took her hand and held it tightly. "Kelly, she lived with this all around her. She's seen things you wouldn't want a baby to see. And it wouldn't be honest to leave out the ugly parts." He gave Kelly a bittersweet smile. "The truth will set you free," he said almost mockingly.

"I'm not so sure that's always true," she retorted, but she saw his point. "Just don't get too graphic, okay?"

"Don't worry." He took a deep breath and continued. "The family was on the run. They had to leave their beautiful plantation behind and hide in the jungle, finding relatives who would take them in. I searched for Angie for days. When I finally found her, we only had a few minutes before—"

His voice caught and he didn't go on, but Kelly thought she understood. She'd read about how he'd been shot. Angie must have been killed at the same time. Kelly's heart broke for him.

"The rebels were pushed out and Angie's family got their plantation back. But Angie's mother blamed me for her daughter's death. I suppose she was right. It was my fault. If she hadn't come out to meet me that day…" Tears filled his eyes.

"Joe."

Kelly reached out to comfort him, but before her hand could grasp his, she realized Mei had come over, too. Toddling on her little chubby legs, she looked at him for a moment, then leaned forward and patted his leg with her hand. Two pats, and she turned and went back to her toys.

Kelly and Joe looked at each other in astonishment, hardly believing what she'd just done. Joe moved as though to go to her, but Kelly held him back.

"Later," she whispered. "Give her time to get used to this."

He nodded, took a deep breath and went on, talking about things he and Angie had done, about what life was like in the Philippines. As he talked, Mei played with her toys, then lay down on the floor and closed her eyes.

"Do you really think any of this is getting through to her?" Joe asked softly.

"Not the way it would to an adult." Kelly sighed. "But I think it's done a lot of good. It's all in the vibes."

He rose and walked over to where his daughter was lying. "There you go, I bored her to death. She's out cold."

"She's asleep." Kelly smiled. "And with babies, that's

usually a good thing." She rose as well. "Come on. Help me put her down in her crib."

"I'll do it," he said, and he bent down and slipped his hands under her neck and her legs. She woke as he lifted her, and her first reaction was to scrunch up her face and try to wrestle free. But Joe didn't let her. He pulled her against his chest and held her tenderly, rocking her and murmuring sweet words. In a moment, she stilled, and then her eyes closed again and she was limp as a noodle. Joe looked at Kelly and grinned.

Kelly was dancing with happiness—but very quietly. Together, they put the baby in her crib and pulled the blanket over her.

"It's going to be okay," Kelly whispered as they tiptoed out of the room. "You'll see. You've done it. Congrats."

"No, you've done it." He stopped, closed the door to the room and pulled her into his arms. "Thank God for you," he said, his voice low and husky. And then he kissed her.

She'd heard of kisses that took you to heaven, and she'd always scorned such talk.

But that was then. This was now.

And now was very different. Maybe it was the powerful maleness of him that did it. Suddenly everything was all senses—touch and smell and taste—and her brain seemed to go to sleep. His mouth on hers felt as hot and lush as black velvet looked, and it wasn't just touching—it was stroking and coaxing and plunging and drawing her out as she'd never been before. She seemed to be floating, and she couldn't feel her legs anymore.

Everything was focused on the kiss. She was living in this incredible sensation, and she never wanted it to stop.

His body was hard and lean and delicious, and she pressed herself against him, hungry to feel him against her breasts, wanting more of him and wanting it harder.

Vaguely, she realized he was saying something, and then he was drawing back. She didn't want him to go. She clung to him with an urgency she didn't know she had in her.

"Whoa, hold on," he said softly, taking her head in his hands and laughing down into her face. "Kelly, Kelly, if we keep this up, we'll be sorry, sweetheart. Let's take it easy for now. Okay?"

"Oh!" Her face turned bright red. "Oh, Joe, I've never…I mean I didn't…"

"Darling, it's quite obvious 'you've never.' And I don't think you're ready yet, either. No matter what that eager body of yours tells you."

She put her hand over her mouth. She'd never been so embarrassed in her life. "Oh Joe, I didn't mean to…"

"I know." He laced fingers with her, smiling at her with a sweet and lingering tenderness. "It's my fault. I got that train started down the track. I didn't know you didn't have any brakes."

"Joe!"

He laughed. "I'm kidding. Come on. Let's go out on the deck and cool off."

She went with him. The moon was out, the sound of the waves a calming backdrop. She looked into the night sky and sighed. If she hadn't already been pretty sure she was in love with him, she knew for sure now.

Kelly changed her plane reservations in the morning, but could add only one day. There was no getting out of going home on Sunday. After all, her job was worth saving.

Mei was beginning to respond to Joe. It was going to take time for her to be as natural with him as he would like, but it was coming along. They spent Saturday at the beach with her and then took her to a kiddie park where she could play on the equipment. They all three seemed to grow closer every minute they spent together.

Joe couldn't believe how happy it made him just to be with Kelly and Mei. But lurking in the background were the decisions he was going to have to make. Was he really a prince? And if so, was he ready to pick up that mantle?

This was a complicated problem. It wasn't as though there was a nice, placid life waiting for him in Ambria. If he wanted to claim his heritage, he was going to have to fight for it. There was a war waiting to be fought. Was he going to feel strongly enough about all this to be a part of that?

He'd been a fighter all his life. His career was based on the warrior creed. He'd assumed that was the only work he was trained in and the only work he would get. He'd had plenty of offers and he thought he'd take one soon.

But what if he could do something better? Something tied to his own heritage, his own destiny? Getting his country back from the evil clan who'd stolen it, the villains who had murdered his parents, the force that cursed his native land.

Wasn't that what his entire career, his entire life, had prepared him for? If he was a prince—and he was becoming more and more certain that he was—it was his duty, wasn't it?

Kelly seemed to think so.

"I've got my boss setting up some meetings for you," she told him that afternoon. "He'll arrange for your DNA test and—"

"Whoa," Joe said, shocked at how quickly this was coming at him. "I haven't said I would do that yet."

"No." She smiled at him sweetly. "But you will. Won't you?"

He melted. It was that smile that did it. This was not good. She could just about get him to do anything, couldn't she?

"I guess it wouldn't hurt to get the facts," he said grudgingly. "But what are these meetings you're talking about?"

"Different officials will be calling to discuss the possibilities with you." She hesitated, then smiled again, taking his hand in hers. "They'll want you to come to Italy."

"How am I going to do that? I can't leave Mei behind."

"Take her with you, of course. They'll find someone to help with that. Don't worry. Very soon, there will be people popping out of the woodwork to help you with everything. Get ready to feel overwhelmed."

He wasn't sure if he liked that prospect, and his eyes were troubled as he looked down at her. "I haven't said I'd do all this yet, you know," he reminded her.

She nodded. "But you will. You have to."

He had to? His natural sense of rebellion was rising up.

"I don't *have* to do anything," he claimed, feeling grumpy. Reaching out, he brushed back the hair from her face and looked at her lips. "Except kiss you. A lot."

She smiled up at him. "Of course," she murmured. "That goes without saying."

So he did.

On Sunday morning, Kelly was preparing to go, and it broke her heart. How was she going to say goodbye to the child who still clung to her neck every time she got the chance? How many mothers and mother surrogates did this baby have to lose in one lifetime?

And then there was Joe. Kelly couldn't even think about that.

Mei was asleep, and she wasn't going to go in and look at her once more. It was time. She turned to Joe.

He came toward her and pulled her into his arms, rocking her and holding her against him.

"Kelly," he said, his voice rough, "I want you to stay."

She closed her eyes. This was so hard. "Joe, you know I can't. I've thought about it long and hard. But I can't."

"Is it your job?"

She nodded, pulling her head back so she could look in his face. "You are Prince Cassius of Ambria and you have to take your place in that system. No matter how much you try to fight it, you belong there. I don't. I would have no place there, no tie, no claim. And anyway, I would lose my job." She shook her head sadly. "I have to look out for my own future."

He groaned. "If you get on that plane, we'll probably never see each other again."

She knew he was right. But it had to be. She stayed with him until she was already behind schedule, and then she finally tore herself away.

"I don't want you to come to the airport," she told him when he offered.

"Why not?"

She looked at him with tragic eyes. "I need to take my rental car back, anyway. I'd rather cut it off here and try to get back into my normal patterns right away. It'll…it'll be easier if I just…"

Her eyes filled with tears and she turned away. "Goodbye, Joe," she said, her voice choked. "Good luck."

"Kelly, wait."

Shaking her head, she kept walking, fighting back the tears.

She heard him coming up behind her, but she was startled when he put his hand on her elbow, pulled her around and took her into his arms.

"Kelly," he said roughly, looking down into her face. "Don't you know that I love you?"

"Joe…"

His mouth on hers was sweet and urgent all at once. She kissed him back, loving him, longing for him, wishing things were different. But they were what they were.

"Oh, Joe," she said brokenly as she clung to him. "I love you, too. But it doesn't matter. We can't…"

"Why can't we?" he said, wiping away her tears with his finger and gazing at her lovingly. "I don't have to be a prince. I don't even want to be one. I'd rather be with you."

"No." Drawing back, she shook her head. "No, Joe. You have to go to Italy. You have to explore your destiny. I couldn't live with myself if I kept you from that. You know you have to do it."

Reaching up, she pressed her fingertips to his lips in one last gesture of affection. "Goodbye," she whispered again. And she turned and left him there.

He didn't say anything at all as he watched her walk to the car. This wasn't like watching Angie die. Not anything close to that. But it hurt almost as badly.

To be or not to be. A prince, that was.

Did he really want to do this thing? Joe wasn't sure. He had now talked to the liaison people Kelly had set up for him, and they wanted him in Italy right away. They claimed they had accommodations ready for him, including servants and child care for Mei. It sounded kind of cushy—one might almost say royal.

Of course, they were expecting him to take a DNA test first thing. That was only reasonable. And he had no doubt what it would show. He was Prince Cassius. He knew that now.

Prince Cassius of the DeAngelis family who had ruled Ambria for hundreds of years. Wow. That was a real kick in the head.

Did he feel royal? Not really. He felt like the same Army Ranger he'd been since he left school. He'd grown up in a working-class household without any thoughts of privilege, and those early lessons would stay with him all his life. Admittedly, this was going to be quite an adjustment for him. Did he want to make it? Was he sure?

He wasn't sure of much of anything right now. His life was in flux and he was caught in the rapids. But there was one truth that he would never waver on—Mei was going to be with him wherever he went, whatever he did. His first priority would always be her. And Angie would always have a central place in his heart.

But there was something else that was becoming more and more important to him, and it centered around a woman with a mop of curly blonde hair and an irrepressible smile—the very woman who had brought all this royal stuff crashing down on him. Kelly. He missed her every minute. How could you miss someone so much who you hadn't even known two weeks ago? Something about her had worked for him from the very beginning. If he had Kelly with him right now, he'd be a lot more sure of what he was doing.

Was he in love with her? He thought back to how it had been with Angie, how he'd fallen hard from the moment he first saw her, how she'd swept up his life into days of passion, weeks of torture when he was away from her, moments of high drama and the awful, final act of destruction. It had been a wild ride, but—except for the ending—he wouldn't have missed a moment of it. Angie was part of him now, and she had left him with Mei, the best present of his life.

The way he felt about Kelly was different, and yet in some ways it was stronger even and more life-changing. She saw into his soul in ways no one else ever had. She could tell him more with a simple glance than anyone else, as well. In the short time she'd been with him, she'd made a lasting impact on them all. Kelly could have been his angel for the long haul, the center of something big and important. If only they'd had a little longer together...

But life didn't stand still and let you take time with decisions. It came at you quickly and you had to be ready to take it on. They wanted him to be a prince. Okay. He'd give it a try. He'd go to the funeral in Piasa. He'd meet the others and check the lay of the land and decide from there.

There was one missing ingredient, though. Something he was going to have to have. He sat down and looked up some numbers on his cell phone. He had a few people to call.

Kelly had been back to work for three days. California seemed like a dream. Had she really been there? Had she really fallen in love with a prince?

Yes, she had. But it was all over now. She had to get back to real life, even though there was a big, black hole in the middle of her soul.

She'd never been in love before. She hadn't realized

how much it was going to hurt to know she could never have Joe, no matter what she did. For the first two days, she'd felt as though her life was over. She was getting better now. She had finally slept the night before, and was actually able to force down some toast for breakfast before coming in. Now she was just trying to retrain herself to focus on her work and not dream all day about a certain golden surfer who was far, far away.

She was typing up a report when Jim came in waving a piece of paper.

"Guess who's going to the funeral?" he said, looking acerbic.

"Oh. Did you get an assignment?"

"No." He waved the paper at her. "You did."

"What?" She frowned. That couldn't be right.

"It says so right here. Better pack your things. They want you in Italy right away."

"Oh my gosh!"

The whole situation was crazy. How had she been chosen? But she didn't want to ask too many questions. She was afraid someone would say, "Hey, why are we sending her, anyway?" and it would be all over. So she kept her head down and made quick preparations, and before she knew it, she was on the plane to Italy.

And all she could think about was Joe. Would she see him? Would she get a glimpse of Mei? Maybe she'd see them at a fancy restaurant, or maybe there would be a parade and they would be in it. If she waved, would they wave back? How hard would that be—to see them passing and have them look right through her? She didn't know if she would be able to stand it.

But she was going. What would be would be. Piasa wasn't a very big town. Surely she would see them somewhere, at some point.

She landed at the airport and took a five-hour taxi ride into the mountains. The town of Piasa looked as if it belonged in the Swiss Alps. It was very quaint and adorable, with chalets and wildflowers everywhere. She almost expected to see Julie Andrews bursting into song every time she looked at the mountains.

Kelly spent the first day getting acclimatized, checking into her hotel, learning where she needed to go to get information, meeting some of the townsfolk. And asking discreetly if anyone knew anything about the lost princes. No one did.

But all in all, it was pretty exciting meeting Ambrians everywhere. The feeling of kinship was strong and there seemed to be a festive spirit in the air. Something was up, that was for sure.

When she finally got back to her hotel room that first night, there was a message from her home office of the Ambrian News Agency, asking why she hadn't contacted her client yet, and giving a number for doing so.

Client? What client? No one had told her there was a specific client involved. But she supposed that must be why she'd received the last-minute assignment, and no one had completed briefing her on what she was expected to do here.

She looked at the clock. It was too late to do anything about it tonight. She would call the number in the morning. With a sigh, she began to get ready for bed.

And then she heard a strange sound. She stopped, holding her breath. Something brushed against her door, and then there was whispering. And finally, a firm knock.

Her heart began to pound. This was an idyllic, picturesque little town, but she knew behind the pretty pictures lurked a perpetual menace. The Granvillis were behind most of the ugly incidents that happened to expatriot Ambrians. Everywhere she'd gone today, people had warned her to be careful.

She went to the door and listened. There was still whispering, but she couldn't make it out.

"Who is it?" she called.

A voice spoke—what sounded almost like a child's voice.

A child's voice. But it couldn't be….

"Mei?" she said, almost whispering herself. Throwing caution to the wind, she ripped the door open.

"Mei!"

There was the darling little girl, high up in Joe's arms, and now shrieking with laughter and clapping her hands. Kelly was so surprised she stood in shocked paralysis, her mouth open.

"Hey, better let us in," Joe advised, his grin wide and his eyes filled with affection. "You'll have your neighbors up in arms at all the noise soon."

"Joe!" She stepped back and herded them in. "I can't believe this. I was hoping I would find you somewhere, and here you are."

"Darn right," he said. "We've been trying to catch

up with you all afternoon. You were supposed to check in as soon as you got here."

She shook her head. "What are you talking about?"

"Didn't you guess? We're your clients—me and Mei. I got your agency to send you. I told them I needed to hire you as my communications director for awhile."

She stared at him, at a loss. Things were happening too fast.

"Hey." He pointed his thumb at his chest. "Meet the new boss. You're all mine now."

As if she hadn't been all along. Kelly started to laugh, and then she stopped herself, afraid she might lapse into hysteria. This was all so crazy.

Then she took a good look at them. Joe was dressed in a gray sweatshirt with a hood, and so was Mei. They looked like versions of how she'd appeared on the beach when Joe had first noticed her.

"Yeah, we're running around town undercover," he told her cheerfully. "Did you bring your sweats with you? You can join us. That'll keep you incognito as we make our way back to the Marbella House, where we're staying." He glanced at his watch. "Mei is up way past her bedtime, but she wanted to help me find you, so here she is."

Kelly shook her head in wonder. "So you two are okay now?" she asked, though she really didn't have to.

"Sure. Look at this." He set Mei down in a chair and knelt before her.

"Okay, Mei. We need to show Kelly your new talents. Show her. What does the pig say?"

Mei wiggled her nose and made a very cute grunting noise.

"What does the doggie say?"

She scrunched up her face and woofed heartily.

"What does the Mei say?"

She threw her arms out and wrapped them around Joe's neck. "Dada!" she cried happily.

Kelly watched with tears in her eyes. "That is the best present I could ever have," she told Joe, snuffling a bit as he stood and wrapped his arms around her.

"Okay," he said, lifting her chin and dropping a sweet kiss on her lips. "Then I guess I'll have to try to better it."

She blinked up at him. "What do you mean?"

He shrugged. "How would you like a royal wedding?"

"But…I'm not getting married."

He looked surprised. "Oh. Funny. I thought you were."

She was frowning. He was teasing her again, wasn't he? "No, I'm not, and it's not funny at all. In fact, I think you're—"

She stopped dead. He had a diamond ring in his hand. As she gaped at him, he went down on one knee and presented it to her. "Kelly Vrosis, would you be my wife?" he asked, his eyes shining with something that looked very much like love.

"Oh!"

He raised one eyebrow. "I was hoping for a yes."

"But...but—" She was utterly flabbergasted. Never in a million years had she expected anything like this.

"I need you with me, Kelly. Mei needs you, too. And the only way I can guarantee that is to marry you."

She laughed. "So what you're proposing is a marriage of convenience. Your convenience."

"You might say that. I'd rather say we were meant for each other and there is no point in delaying the inevitable."

Her smile could have warmed the room. "I like that kind of talk."

"And your answer is?"

"Yes! Oh, yes!"

"Dada!" Mei chimed in, clapping her hands.

Joe scooped her up and they had a three-way hug, a family at last.

* * * * *

Don't miss the exciting continuation of Raye Morgan's The Lost Princes of Ambria in next month's CROWN PRINCE, PREGNANT BRIDE! from Harlequin Romance.

MILLS & BOON

DECEMBER 2010 HARDBACK TITLES

ROMANCE

HISTORICAL

MEDICAL™

MILLS & BOON

DECEMBER 2010 LARGE PRINT TITLES

ROMANCE

The Pregnancy Shock	Lynne Graham
Falco: The Dark Guardian	Sandra Marton
One Night...Nine-Month Scandal	Sarah Morgan
The Last Kolovsky Playboy	Carol Marinelli
Doorstep Twins	Rebecca Winters
The Cowboy's Adopted Daughter	Patricia Thayer
SOS: Convenient Husband Required	Liz Fielding
Winning a Groom in 10 Dates	Cara Colter

HISTORICAL

Rake Beyond Redemption	Anne O'Brien
A Thoroughly Compromised Lady	Bronwyn Scott
In the Master's Bed	Blythe Gifford
Bought: The Penniless Lady	Deborah Hale

MEDICAL™

The Midwife and the Millionaire	Fiona McArthur
From Single Mum to Lady	Judy Campbell
Knight on the Children's Ward	Carol Marinelli
Children's Doctor, Shy Nurse	Molly Evans
Hawaiian Sunset, Dream Proposal	Joanna Neil
Rescued: Mother and Baby	Anne Fraser

MILLS & BOON®

JANUARY 2011 HARDBACK TITLES

ROMANCE

Hidden Mistress, Public Wife	Emma Darcy
Jordan St Claire: Dark and Dangerous	Carole Mortimer
The Forbidden Innocent	Sharon Kendrick
Bound to the Greek	Kate Hewitt
The Secretary's Scandalous Secret	Cathy Williams
Ruthless Boss, Dream Baby	Susan Stephens
Prince Voronov's Virgin	Lynn Raye Harris
Mistress, Mother...Wife?	Maggie Cox
With This Fling...	Kelly Hunter
Girls' Guide to Flirting with Danger	Kimberly Lang
Wealthy Australian, Secret Son	Margaret Way
A Winter Proposal	Lucy Gordon
His Diamond Bride	Lucy Gordon
Surprise: Outback Proposal	Jennie Adams
Juggling Briefcase & Baby	Jessica Hart
Deserted Island, Dreamy Ex!	Nicola Marsh
Rescued by the Dreamy Doc	Amy Andrews
Navy Officer to Family Man	Emily Forbes

HISTORICAL

Lady Folbroke's Delicious Deception	Christine Merrill
Breaking the Governess's Rules	Michelle Styles
Her Dark and Dangerous Lord	Anne Herries
How To Marry a Rake	Deb Marlowe

MEDICAL™

Sheikh, Children's Doctor...Husband	Meredith Webber
Six-Week Marriage Miracle	Jessica Matthews
St Piran's: Italian Surgeon, Forbidden Bride	Margaret McDonagh
The Baby Who Stole the Doctor's Heart	Dianne Drake

1210 Gen Std L

JANUARY 2011 LARGE PRINT TITLES

ROMANCE

A Stormy Greek Marriage	Lynne Graham
Unworldly Secretary, Untamed Greek	Kim Lawrence
The Sabbides Secret Baby	Jacqueline Baird
The Undoing of de Luca	Kate Hewitt
Cattle Baron Needs a Bride	Margaret Way
Passionate Chef, Ice Queen Boss	Jennie Adams
Sparks Fly with Mr Mayor	Teresa Carpenter
Rescued in a Wedding Dress	Cara Colter

HISTORICAL

Vicar's Daughter to Viscount's Lady	Louise Allen
Chivalrous Rake, Scandalous Lady	Mary Brendan
The Lord's Forced Bride	Anne Herries
Wanted: Mail-Order Mistress	Deborah Hale

MEDICAL™

Dare She Date the Dreamy Doc?	Sarah Morgan
Dr Drop-Dead Gorgeous	Emily Forbes
Her Brooding Italian Surgeon	Fiona Lowe
A Father for Baby Rose	Margaret Barker
Neurosurgeon . . . and Mum!	Kate Hardy
Wedding in Darling Downs	Leah Martyn